WALL STREET JOURNAL & *USA TODAY* BESTSELLING AUTHOR

SAPPHIRE KNIGHT

Sterling

Cover Design: CT Cover Creations

Editing: Editing Done Write

Format: N.E. Henderson

This book is a work of fiction. The names, characters, places, and incidents are products of the writer's imagination or have been used fictitiously and are not to be construed as real. Any resemblance to persons, living or dead, actual events, locales or organizations is entirely coincidental.

Dedication

For women out there finding their voices.

When a man says he'll do anything for a woman,
he means fight bad guys and kill stormtroopers,
not vacuum or wash dishes.
-Yoda Meme

I open the thin door of my trailer, stepping back with it. The stairs leading up are rickety and don't have a railing. I should nail together a few two-by-fours or something, but I keep forgetting. It's usually not a big deal unless I'm hammered off my ass from partying with Ruin. I'm shirtless in a pair of gray sweatpants, having been chilling on the couch fucking around on my cell. My DMs have been blowing up since going into the porn business. Granted, no one knows my true identity. Can't have that being affiliated with the club. Regardless, thirsty bitches have been hitting up my fake profile left and right.

I meet the tearful blue gaze belonging to Leigh, Ruin's younger sister. She's torn up over something and it has a protective streak rearing inside me. She's not a crier. She hasn't been since she was a kid and we teased her relentlessly. Her irises flick over me briefly before her tormented gaze lands on mine. She's been crying for a while. "Sterling," falls from her lips in a broken whisper. The sound wounds me.

Fuck.

"Can I come in?" she asks after a beat of me staring, unsure of what to do with her. It's not a true question. She's always welcome here, as is Ruin, and she knows as much.

I take another step back, offering her more room. I expect her to trail past me to the couch, maybe snatch up the remote or grab a drink from the fridge. I'm stunned when she approaches me, wrapping her arms around my bare torso. She buries her head under my chin and sobs. I enclose my arms around her in a hug, squeezing her to my frame. Leigh is never this emotional and it has me at a loss of what to do.

My brow scrunches as I stare out the open door. "Leigh?" I have no idea what to think. Is someone hurt? "Is Ruin all right? What's going on?" He was fine earlier. I'd spoken to him, of course, making sure they didn't need me at the club. We never go long without hitting each other up.

She nods, tears tracking over her high cheekbones. "He's fine," she sniffles. "With his chick."

"Your parents?" I ask to be sure.

"E-everyone's okay. They're just busy." Her shoulders bounce with the shrug. Leigh's the club princess, No one is ever too busy for her. She's too kindhearted to want to put anyone out over her feelings, so she doesn't bother them. She's not fooling me with her excuses.

I exhale in some small dose of relief. It still doesn't explain why she's so torn up and here at my place. "Talk to me. You've got my head spinnin'." She's covered in tears and dirt, and it has me ready to lose my shit. I keep one arm around her shoulders while closing the door behind her. "Let's sit." I nod to the couch and lead her to it. She perches on the edge, close enough our knees nearly brush, never breaking my gaze.

"I was walking Duke." Her voice cuts out at the mention of her dog. She swallows, drawing in a quick breath, then continues, "A-and a car came around the curve in the road."

No. This can't be where I think it's headed. Fuck. Chaos should be the one sitting in my spot right now, or even Ruin...but here I am. Christ, this will no doubt have to be dealt with, and I'm not exactly in the position to be calling any shots when it comes to her.

"He was on his leash, not that he ever needed it."

I nod, aware of his training, and to keep her going. My chest is tight inside, my gut flipping. If she's this messed up, whatever happened damn sure isn't anything good and I know I won't like it. Leigh may not be my sister or my girl, but she's important to me. She always has been.

"I moved off the road, but the car swerved towards us. T-they hit my Duke." Her lip does this little tremble and it cuts me deep.

"Motherfucker," I breathe the curse angrily. My jaw clenches as my teeth grit to hold back the demands I want to make. I need to know who the fuck this was and how I can find them. What happens after that is between me, them, and my maker.

"I screamed at them, and then at Duke as well, once I realized he wasn't moving." She's shedding more tears and my chest aches at her being this torn up. She loved that fucking dog, Chaos had him specially trained to protect her, along with everything else.

"You get a plate number or anything specific about the vehicle?" I need every ounce of information she's got. There's no way this was merely a coincidental accident. Could it be someone after family members of the club? Were they after her specifically, being she's prez's daughter? We already had to worry over Tyra. Thankfully, Poe and Ruin are able to help protect her.

"I know who it was," she admits, teeth sinking into her lower lip. She bites down on the rosy, swollen, plump flesh before sharing, "It was Bruce Darington."

Oh. I know Bruce all right. We went to school with the motherfucker. I was a year older than him and Ruin, but I was around when he tried starting shit with Ru. It didn't work out so well for him when my best friend laid into his ass. Looks like I'll be getting my turn as well after this bullshit. There's no way in hell he'll get off scot-free without feeling the repercussions. I'll see to it myself. I may be a prospect, my ass belonging to the club, but it doesn't mean I can't cave somebody's face in for some bullshit.

"This is wrong, Leigh. You shouldn't have had to deal with this, especially not alone." I reach out, taking her fingers in mine, and lightly squeeze in comfort. "Let's load up, Boo. I'll go with you to where Duke's at and help you bury him. I know you loved him and it's only right we bury him so you have a spot for him. I won't leave you alone through this, you have my word."

Her chin wobbles and I can no longer take it. I lean in, wrapping her in my embrace once more. She shakes her head. "I already took care of it."

I pull back enough to stare down at her adorable dirt-smudged face. I use my thumb to swipe it away from her cheek. "You dug the hole and buried your dog by yourself?"

She nods. This chick blows my fucking mind, I swear.

"Fuck." She's so goddamn strong. She'd have to be, coming from Chaos, and then having Ruin for a brother, but damn, this is next-level bad bitch. "I would've helped you." I give her another squeeze and drop my arms. "Anytime when it comes to something like this."

"I wanted to do it. I needed the time with him so I could say good-bye."

"You didn't hurt yourself?" Digging a hole for that big-ass dog is no joke. She's lucky if she didn't pull something. I have to make sure she's not physically injured, first and foremost.

"No. I'm okay," she says with a yawn and swipes at the wetness coating her cheeks.

"How about we watch a movie. I don't want you alone right now." I lightly graze her cheek. "You've got a bit of dirt here," I mention since it still hasn't come off. She's kinda fucking adorable with it, and I shouldn't be thinking of her in that sense. She's Ruin's sister, not some normal chick.

"Okay, can I clean up? And can we watch it in your room? Your couch is too small for both of us."

"Sure. What are you in the mood for?"

"How about 'Homefront'? I could use some action."

I take her words in a different manner but refrain from teasing her. Now's obviously not the time for it. Besides, I don't want to make her uncomfortable in that sense.

"You got it. I'll set it all up." I head for my bedroom while she goes to my bathroom.

I'm lying on my bed, movie paused, texting Ruin that Leigh's here with me and asking if he knows Bruce's address when she climbs in bed beside me. I hit play and toss my phone to the side before looking up. Her hair's twisted in a towel that's arranged on top of her head, with another towel wrapped around her naked body.

I swallow, throat drier than a moment ago. "Uh," I manage, my voice coming out gruff.

She offers a small smile. "My clothes are filthy. Can I borrow something?"

My head jerks. I cough out, "Sure. Anything."

She heads for my closet, rifling through it. After a beat, she takes out one of my favorite shirts and pulls it over her head, the towel leaves her body once my shirt reaches the bottom of her ass cheeks. My cock begins to harden so I frog my leg, yelping into my pillow. It's the only thing I can do at this moment that'll work quickly, aside from hitting my dick.

She glances over her shoulder, asking, "You okay?" Then proceeds to pull a pair of my sweatpants over her shapely thighs.

Do women not have any idea how goddamn sexy they are when they wear our clothes? Christ Almighty, this chick is going to be the death of me and I haven't even done anything!

"Fine. Muscle spasm, from riding my 750 too much," I mutter, blaming my motorcycle, but she's already distracted. She riffles through my basket of clean clothes, grabbing some socks before making her way to my bed. She sits on the side, pulling socks on her feet, while I stare at her like a psycho dipshit who's never been around a chick before. I do porn, for fuckssake, and yet here I am getting a stiffy over my best friend's sister I've known my entire life. Real fucking smart, said no one ever.

She scoots backward, swinging her legs on the bed, and I hit play on the movie, relaxing back in my pillows. I get into the movie, finally feeling more like my usual self and not so conflicted by

Leigh upset. Her mood has to be the reason why I was paying more attention to her earlier. It explains it, my protective instinct taking over and then seeing her in only a towel, I mean, I'm a red-blooded male after all. Anyone else witnessing her like that would have their dick in mind as well.

Her head hits the pillow beside mine and I clear my throat. "Your father is like an uncle to me. I've known him my entire life," I inform Leigh needlessly. "Our fathers are best friends, basically brothers separated at birth."

With a jolt of her shoulders, she snuggles in closer and murmurs, "Yes, and our mothers are friends, growing close enough to call each other family."

Which is exactly why I brought this up in the first place, as a reminder. *My reminder*. "I've stood next to your brother since we were in diapers. He's my closest friend."

"As have I."

"Excuse me?" I say, tilting my head down to meet her gaze. She's lying next to me in my bed, and it'd be too easy to have her wrapped in my embrace. I'm an idiot if I don't put a stop to this, right now before it ever has a chance to begin.

"I've stood next to you as well. You've always been either at my side or had my back."

"You're Ruin's sister. Of course I have," I reason, although I do consider her a friend of mine, aside from being my best friend's younger sister.

"You know that's not the only reason. You're close to my brother, but admit it, we have our own friendship."

She's reading my mind and I can't have that. She can't realize that I'm looking at her in an entirely unfriend-like manner...I'm seeing her as one hundred percent woman. Ruin will attempt to kick my ass with this. I nod. "We do. I won't ever deny the truth." Or that she's the club princess and her father would bury me six feet in the ground. He'd probably pour concrete over the top as well, just to make a point.

"Thank you, Sterling. I was a mess when I got here and you didn't hesitate to let me in."

"I would never turn you away."

"I know," she whispers, her voice sounding a touch off. She's still upset over what happened, with good reason. I can't believe that motherfucker killed her dog. Only a piece of shit would purposefully swerve for someone's dog and then laugh about it. Fury builds inside me with every moment I think about what went down. Leigh didn't deserve any of this being thrown in her direction, and I'll see to it that punishment is doled out. That much I can promise.

I WAKE TO THE SOUND OF A LAWNMOWER. IT'S DAYLIGHT BUT MUST BE FAIRLY early. This is Georgia. It's hotter than sin this far down south, so people mow when the rest of us normal folk are still attempting to sleep. There's a soft, warm body tucked up next to mine, a head on my chest. It takes a moment for me to get my bearings about me and realize I didn't bring a chick home with me last night. The fragrance of my shampoo floats up, and I inhale deep. It smells good, clean, and even better knowing my scent is coming from Leigh's dirty blonde locks. She shifts, one hand tucked between us while the other sprawls out over my chest.

I can't believe I fell asleep. I cast my gaze on the TV. It's black. I have it set on a timer, too lazy to turn it off most nights. Fuck. Leigh must've fallen asleep around the same time I did. I can't believe she stayed the night here, and in my bed no less. We're friends. It shouldn't bother me, but it does. I know what Ruin would think and how he'd react if he showed up right now. The last thing I'd ever want to do is break his trust in any way. Nah...this is Leigh. He'd believe me if I told him nothing happened. It'd look suspicious, but he knows I wouldn't lie to him like that.

"In This Moment" blares from my nightstand as Leigh's ringtone blows up the quiet room. It may as well be a warning bell, as it has me jumping out of my bed, heading for my bathroom. The lyrics repeat as the phone rings a few more times before eventually going silent. I need my space so I head for the kitchen to get the coffee going.

Leigh eventually makes her way out of my room, helping herself to the fresh coffee before joining me on the couch. "Thank you for yesterday," she begins.

"It was nothing. You shouldn't have been alone." I already texted Ruin about Leigh being here upset because of Duke. He needed to be made aware of what happened, and I'd rather he know she's over here through me, versus Leigh mentioning it and him wondering why I never did.

"I'm not a little girl anymore, Sterling."

"I never said that."

"No, but I can see the way you're looking at me. I'm an adult you know...I'm just upset over Duke."

I nod, not saying anything in response. She has no idea about the way I've truly been looking at her, and I can say it's not anything close to what she's describing. Chaos would gut me if he could read my mind right now—or yesterday, for that matter. She's upset and I've got my damn cock clouding my thoughts.

"I'm going to go. Mom and Dad should be back from Atlanta by now, and I need to let them know I buried Duke on their property." She sniffles, quickly wiping away a stray tear, and stands. She sets her cup on the bar between the living room and kitchen. "I'll wash your clothes and bring them back."

I swallow and nod, standing. My clothes have never looked better before. "I'll hold you to it. I like that shirt. Make sure you use those scent things."

"The laundry scent beads."

I shrug. "Whatever you put in Ruins, I want in mine."

She shakes her head, rolling her eyes. "I haven't done his laundry in so long. Me and Mom had to figure out something to do since he smelled like sweaty boy all the time." It brings a smile to her face, and that's all the reassurance I need that she'll be okay. Leighs a strong bitch and seeing her otherwise is alarming.

She heads for the front door and I jolt up to open it for her. I may be a biker and grew up a club brat, but it doesn't mean I don't have manners. "Drive safe. Call me if you have any sort of trouble."

She flashes a grateful smile in my direction and I swear it lights up something inside me. "I'll be fine, but on the off chance something does, I will call."

"Good," I grunt, watching her ass as she steps down my rickety stairs. I really need to get those fuckers fixed. "Later."

"Bye, Sterling," she calls as her booty sways. I swear to God that woman is going to be the death of whatever dude she finally lands. She's trouble, but then you have Chaos, Ruin, and me watching her back as well.

Once she pulls out of the driveway, I grab my phone. I quickly shoot another text to Ruin and jog for my room. I grab the first pair of jeans I find, a white T-shirt, and my boots. I tug them on, grab a baseball cap, flip it backward, and slide it on. I stuff my phone in my pocket, snatch my wallet, shades, and keys, and stride out the door. Leigh's had plenty of time to leave, so she won't know what I'm doing. The last thing we need is for her to get involved any more than she already is.

I glance around out of habit, seeing that she's indeed left my place. I had to wait her out all night, but no more. I have this fuckface's address and I plan on paying him a visit. I hop in the destroyer-gray Charger that used to belong to my pops. He gave it to me when he found out my mom had raced another member along the highway that's out front of the club. Mom's been known to be a bit wild, and Dad's crazy, so I guess you can say I come by my own hellish ways through them.

I crank the ignition, the engine roaring to life, and Marilyn Manson has the speakers screaming and the subwoofers rattling everybody's thin-ass windows in the trailer park. This car is the only warning Bruce will have that I'm coming for him. Everybody in this shithole town knows this Charger belonged to Bash, the Kings of Carnage's vice president, and he's a bad motherfucker.

Shifting into gear, I release the clutch and peel out of the trailer park. I'm furious inside. The emotion has been festering in my chest ever since Leigh told me what happened. The feelings have grown until this all-consuming rage nearly blinds me. The illegal straight pipes roar as I gun the gas, flying down the pavement, not giving a fuck about anyone's hearing or comfort.

I fishtail, pulling into Bruce's yard, the lot being mostly dirt and dead grass. I pop the car into park, leaving it running and the driver's side door open as I hop out. The thunder of motorcycles doesn't escape me as I storm towards the front door. Ruin must've read my last text and grabbed some guys. Hell, if he told Chaos then there's a chance it may be the prez heading my way to take his vengeance.

I twist the unlocked handle on the front door and then lay into it with a solid kick. It flings open, smacking into the assclown standing next to it. He bellows in pain, the door distracting him from me. It's all the time I need as I snatch him from behind the neck, grip clamped hard as fuck, as I drag his punk-ass outside.

"What the hell?" he screams, and I bellow in rage. I toss him to the ground and my boot finds his ribs with my next kick.

"You went for Leigh? You have a motherfuckin' death wish?" I lash out at him again with another strike. The bikes rumble into the driveway as I'm leaping on top of Bruce, going to town on him with my fists. I get a few hits in when strong arms wrap around me, dragging me backward.

"Calm down, son," my pops barks as Ruin lunges for Bruce next. North is quick to yank him off, but Ru still manages to bust Bruce's eyebrow open. He's dragged back to the bikes, while Chaos steps over the scum sprawled out on the ground.

"You should've let me keep going," I huff, chest heaving. "He needs to be taught a lesson."

"And take the honor from Chaos? I think not. It's his daughter. He should have the chance to dole out the punishment."

I keep the retort to myself that he wouldn't know about it had I not texted Ruin in a fit of rage. I thought I may end up killing Bruce and needed someone to know what the hell was going on. I'm still a prospect, so I have to keep my mouth shut. Twenty-two and been prospecting for the Kings of Carnage for what feels like damn near my entire life. Pops and Chaos don't see it that way though, the stubborn old mules.

My father is too important. He's the club VP and an arms dealer. He used to peddle drugs back in the day but got out of it when I came into the picture. Anyhow, he's been teaching me the ways of the club since I was a toddler, but once I officially started prospecting, he brought me into his gun business as well. It's not a typical career you hear of a father passing on to his son, but we use what we've got.

"You and Ruin stick him in your trunk," Chaos orders and Dad agrees, releasing his firm grip from my shoulder. I shoot my best friend a look that says he better not hurt the fucker without me. He sends me a grin and I can read the look immediately. He's on the same page as I am. North stands next to our fathers, watching us with his hands on his hips.

"You gonna call Leigh?" I ask as I grab Bruce's feet and Ruin goes for the arms. Bruce has been knocked the fuck out, no doubt done by Chaos while I was busy watching Ruin get torn from the bastard.

"I'll text her on the way to the bike. Can't just yet or they'll know something's up."

"Right," I press a button under the trunk to release the latch. We stuff the body back there, wrapping his legs and arms with some bungee cords to make it's more difficult for him should he wake up. I don't want Leigh to know I went after Bruce just yet. She's barely had time to process the death of her dog. I was trying to keep her out of it. She's Ruin's sister though, he'd know what she can handle more so than me, I suppose.

"I appreciate you being there for her last night. Chaos won't say shit, but he's wrecked inside he wasn't around to handle it."

I shrug it off. "No biggie. We're family," I mutter, and he dips his head, agreeing. I need to keep reminding myself that family doesn't look at 'family' the way I was at Leigh last night.

Chin up, you poor little soul, one day you will make that dream a reality, and we'll see that smile again.
-Pinterest Meme

Sterling

I need the cash, so I do what pays the bills. Not that this line of work is tough by any means. Hell, everyone I know would dream of doing what we do. I remove my clothes, flashing a confident grin at the chick in front of me—Bambi. Her gaze is greedy as it takes in my body. I'm not ripped by any means, but I know I look good. I've been told I've got sexy lips and chicks love my hair for some reason.

"I've heard you're a wild boy." She tosses out a flirty smile, acting as if she doesn't already know what my cock feels like. We've been through this before. She's one of the females I don't mind fucking repeatedly on camera.

I wink, my mouth twisting up at the word boy. "*Man*, baby. I'm a wild man and I'm about to light your pussy up like it's the Fourth of July. Our viewers won't be able to hold themselves back from touching themselves."

The comment elicits a giggle and eases the bit of awkwardness lingering between us since the last time we fucked. I was expecting it to be a little weird. It always is. We meet up, and someone records us having sex or whatever we're supposed to be doing that day to change shit up. Usually it's Ruin behind the monitors and vice-versa. We've grown comfortable with each other over time, since we were all up in each other's shit in the beginning. Don't knock a cell cam until you've tried it on porn sites. People will pay for shit made on any camera if it's good. When we had the threesome with his chick, it was a damn goldmine. People couldn't watch it fast enough it seemed.

"I told you last time your subscribers would double, didn't I? Was I wrong?"

She grins and shakes her head. "You were right. I've been making a nice side hustle on our fans account doing sexy story time."

"Oh, you naughty, naughty little porn star," I comment, and she laughs again. The tension filters out some more as our work chemistry comes to the surface.

Porn's nothing like I was expecting it to be. It's not the same as coming home fucked up and slamming into a chick until you pass out. This shit is all recorded while being sober. Well, aside from a bit of weed I smoke prior. It helps me chill out and go with the flow. Ruin's smart. I have to give it to him for coming up with the idea to not only fill our pockets but the club's as well. We'd be off screwing around and fucking chicks regardless. May as well get some paper doing it. KOC gets half of the profits for the club, but we still manage to make a fairly decent cut for ourselves. I also get a little kickback from the runs I do with Dad so I usually do all right.

The door opens, light filling the room and drawing my attention as it's dim in here until we get into position and the lighting shifted to where the camera needs it. We rarely get anyone stopping by, unless it's a brother or prospect from the club. It's hard to get chicks to relax well enough when there are too many folks watching you fuck them. Sure, we've got a few who get off on the added attention and the presence amps them up. Then there're females like the one I'm fixing to sink into. Sweet ol' Bambi's a touch on the skittish side.

She steps behind me as the light fades with the door closing again. It's a bright enough setting for me to make out Leigh's stiff frame. Her eyes take me in from top to bottom, eventually pinning on my exposed abdomen. I clear my throat, my cock suddenly not so excited about what's fixing to go down. I don't want to fuck this bitch in front of Leigh. Friend or not, it's weird. She'll look at me differently if she watches. I already know it, and that's not something I want to go through or put her through either.

"Leigh?" The grunt eventually leaves my lips, low and gruff. Why is she even here? This is the last place she belongs. She should be home or at the smoothie shop, staying safe and out of trouble.

"Hey. I saw your bike out there, but..." she trails off.

I nod. "Yeah. You good? Need anything?"

She skirts her gaze around the room to land on Ruin. "My brother asked me to drop off his stuff he left in my car."

"Oh, right," I mutter, my forehead screwing up with what she's said. Since when does he have her come here? She's the club princess, doesn't belong anywhere near this place. Does he have suspicions about me and Leigh? Nah, that's ludicrous. He's my best friend, and besides, there's nothing between me and his sister. The thought of her here around this sort of thing still angers me.

I shoot a hard look in Ruin's direction. "You trying to get Chaos to gut us?" I ask him, not wanting him to know I'm irritated for any other reason with Leigh being here.

Leigh scowls but doesn't comment. Rather, she trots her perfect booty to her brother and sets the duffle bag at his feet. "I better be bringing you a bag of drugs and not plastic dicks."

Crow and Saint cut up at her remark, but I scowl. "She needs to go. We're trying to make some cash."

Her hand goes to rest on her side and she pops her hip out a bit. I can read the attitude from a mile away. Fuck my life. I should've let Ruin deal with her and kept my mouth shut. "Maybe I want to make some money too," she tosses the gauntlet out.

Ruin and I both reply simultaneously, "Nope. Not happening."

"Fuck no," he repeats, glowering at her.

She folds her arms. "Fine, then I'll just hang out awhile and see how this whole production works. I may be helpful, you never know."

"Not happening," I echo my previous comment, and thankfully, Ruin agrees immediately.

"I asked you to drop my shit. Now you're just acting like a brat."

Her gaze twinkles. "I'm sure someone here wouldn't mind me staying around."

I point my scowl at Crow and Saint, but they look as lost as I'm currently feeling.

"The fuck? Who?" Ruin demands, and I'm all ears. I want to hear this too. I dare a motherfucker to speak up.

She looks to me, but I keep my trap shut. Eventually, her shoulders bounce. "I was just saying someone, not anyone in particular."

"Sure. Sterling's right. Chaos will go ballistic if you're here, and I'm not trying to die for you today over a goddamn porno. Let Sterling and Bambi get to it. They've both got lives to get back to."

She shoots me a wounded glare then spins on her heel, storming towards the door, perfect ass encased in a pair of black velvet pants that'd bring a man to his knees. She pauses long enough to send me a lingering look that has my stomach flopping like a dying fish. Fuck. She's out the door in the next breath, and there's no way my cocks coming out to play after that.

Fucking shit. This can't be happening right now. I turn to Ruin, exasperated. He reads me easily enough. "Pull your dick out and let's do this."

I shake my head, moving for my shoes. "I need to check on Boo."

He rolls his eyes, but nods. "Lot of drama with your ass lately."

I flash a grin and flip him off on my way out. "Leigh!" I shout when I get the front door open and catch her sliding into her driver's seat. Damn it. She's upset, although she'd never let any of us know it. I've known her my entire life. Fairly sure she can't hide this shit from me anymore.

"Wait!" Her car starts and I manage to put my hands on her open windowsill.

"I need to go," she huffs, not looking at me. Something's changed between us, and I'm not exactly sure what it is or when it happened. I'm definitely feeling it right now, as well as back there in that room.

"Will you look at me?" I ask, exasperated. She doesn't, and it's making me feel like I swallowed something sour. "Fine," I bite out.

I exhale, rubbing my hand through my unruly hair. She stubbornly remains quiet, and it's enough to drive a man insane. I normally have patience with her, but her upset with me has me all out of whack. "You don't want to talk to me, then I'll stop wasting your time," I bark out, the irritation coming out of left field. I have no right to be like this towards her. I shouldn't care, yet I do. The last thing I want is for her to be hurt or upset over something, especially if there's a way for me to fix it.

"Sterling," she begins as soon as I turn away. She quietly stares out her windshield before flashing a quick glance my way. "I have to go," she eventually murmurs.

With a jerk of my chin, I leave. I tried. It's all I can do. If she doesn't want to speak to me, then so be it. I have a job waiting for me. Unlike Leigh, the thirsty bitches around here won't hesitate if I should give them any of my attention. I hear the car drive away, not giving her the satisfaction of seeing me glance back.

Could this be over Bruce? I'm not sure what anyone told her about what concerns him and his whereabouts. Ruin was going to text her that we had Bruce and she didn't have to worry again, but who knows if she was informed it was me who hunted his ass down. Hardly a reason to be upset with me. Not like I killed him or anything. I wanted to, don't get me wrong, but once he was loaded into my car, Chaos was all over my ass about him. No matter if Ruin and I had wanted to give Leigh the option of taking her vengeance out on him, her father wasn't having it.

"Hey, Sterling," Asia's velvety voice greets, snapping me away from my thoughts. She's another of the girls we shoot these films with, and she's thirsty as fuck. I could see it from day one that she's a stage-five clinger. Ain't nobody have time for that shit, especially being a biker. We do commitment like we buy new boots—never fuckin' happens unless absolutely necessary. "You just get here?"

I shake my head. "Nah, I've been around for a bit. You filming today?"

"I thought I'd stop by to see if there was partying tonight. You guys know how to have fun and show a girl a good time."

My lips kick up. "That so? Who've you been letting show you that good time?" I ask like I'm interested, but the only thing I care about is if she's still clean. Ruin runs a tight ship about that sort of thing. It's not my business personally, unless we're fucking, but he needs to be made aware if Asia's been going around outside of their agreement.

"Oh, you know, just you guys. I promised to be a good girl, unless you wanted me bad?" she poses it as a question when I know it's merely her offering up whatever I want. No, thank you. I only have her on camera when necessary. I'm not an idiot looking to put a property patch on her ass, even though I know it's exactly what she wants.

I'm too young to be looking for anything serious. Besides, I'm having far too much fun out playing the field. There's also the small disclosure of what I do to make a living, working for Porn Kings and prospecting for the Kings of Carnage MC. I highly doubt there'd be many women out there okay with me fucking other chicks and selling guns with my pops. To make things even more difficult, it's not like I could tell a female what I do for the club anyhow. My life is one big secret to the outside world, and it's gotta stay that way for the long haul.

KOC has a decent chance at bringing in some paper with the fresh blood moving in to be patched, such as myself. We're damn near cash cows, until one of us gets pinched and we're forced to do some time behind bars. My father has always preached about how it's important to keep my hands clean for as long as possible. Can't blame the old man. His life is the club, aside from his family, and he'd rather me go into guns with him than my younger brother Stryker.

Stryker is smart but also tends to be a bit of a show-off. Determined to live up to his namesake, he's always getting into fights and stirring shit up when he's bored. Pops has had him training since he was a kid, and at eighteen, he's foaming at the mouth at the possibility of booking bigger fights and prospecting for the club. I keep trying to get him to understand that Chaos won't want him around if he's stirring up fights and bringing heat on the club. The fucker will learn eventually he'll only get in with club-sanctioned fights.

My sister is the opposite, with her calm disposition and genius-level intelligence. I don't know what mom was drinking in her Kool-Aid when she was pregnant with Sawyer, but I wish she'd shared the love with the rest of us. I have a sibling who can fight his way out of anything and another who can think her way out of it, then there's me. Average, run-of-the-mill Sterling Strauss Spade, who films porn and sells guns. I'd be the black sheep of the family if it weren't for my dad and the brothers. The club has been the center of my life for as long as I can remember. I eat, sleep, and breathe the Kings of Carnage MC and wouldn't have it any other way.

Luckily, so does Ruin, or else I doubt we'd be as close as we are. Being only a year apart, we went to school together and always had each other's backs. He gave me my first tattoo when he started learning from Poe and has been around doing dumb shit right along beside me. When I turned eighteen, Poe had a girl in doing piercings, and Ruin egged me on to get one done since I thought the chick was hot. Well, one thing led to another, and that's how my Jacob's ladder came into play and why the new prospects believe Sterling is my road name. Little do they know it's my actual name that my father came up with due to the color of my eyes. I'll keep that bit to myself though. The dick piercing makes me sound more like a badass who didn't back down from having my cock pierced multiple times.

"You good?" Crow sticks his head out the bedroom door, looking at me like I've lost my mind. They're all probably wondering why I left after Leigh, but I won't be saying shit about it. I never share my business, unless it's with Ruin. Everybody else can wonder all they want.

"Fine, man. Just chatting it up with Asia. She's here to see if anyone wants to party." I raise my brow, silently warning him not to say shit about what we have planned. She'll have his ass wifey'ing her in a heartbeat if she gets the chance.

"Uh..." He clears his throat. "Just working like usual," he mumbles, and I skirt past him, flashing an amused grin. Her curves and tits will have him stumbling over his words. Hell, she had that same influence on me the first time I saw her too. Then the silent, bright warning light flashed before me, and I've kept my dick in my pants around her since.

I enter the room to find Bambi buck-ass naked, making doe eyes at Ruin. He must've been filming her touching herself since I was absent. I shuck my boots, jeans, and boxer briefs, then grab for the baby oil. I use it sparingly. I learned the hard way the first time how fucking hard it is to get this shit off. Rubbing it over my palms, I glide it across my chest and abdomen. I wipe my hands on the small towel before giving my cock a few tugs while staring at Bambi. I can't use the oil on my length or it'll jack up the condom—we learned that much early on.

Wish I could say I had her in my mind's eye, but it's another spicy chick filling my thoughts. She doesn't belong in my fantasies, but there's nothing I can do at the moment when I need my length standing at attention. I know it'll never happen between us, so I let my imagination play out. Just picturing her waiting for me, turned on and ready, has the tip of my cock beading with precum.

I remain still, hand on my cock, while our makeup chick and Ruin's girl, Tyra, paints my face. She's cool, Poe's daughter, and happens to be super artistic. I fucked her a while back with Ruin, hence the threesome video that went viral. She was good, but we didn't click like her and my boy did. Thankfully, he knows I'm not into her past the shared fuck we had, so he has no reason to be weird about me being naked in front of her. She turns my face into a sick-as-fuck skull, dusting some powder shit on, then spraying it down with setting spray so I don't sweat the shit off. It's itchy as fuck, but I've grown used to it. She airbrushes our faces and bodies at times too, but this one is a quick session, so no need for the extra detail.

There's also a mask I use at times as well. It's even quicker, but if we're doing certain frames then it's better to have the paint on. Ruin signals once Tyra's finished hiding my identity well enough for our video. I give him a thumbs up. He nods the go-ahead to signal he's recording, and I step into the frame.

"Heard you've been wanting to play on the dark side," I growl, my pitch deep to help disguise my voice as well. It's not a big deal if you're moaning and grunting, but for this part, the stories and what not, I always attempt to make my voice lower. My gaze finds Bambi's naked, lithe form, eagerly waiting for me. She's just another hole to fill, another payday to collect on, and that's the only way I'll ever see her.

"Oh no!" she shrieks, going over the lines we'd rehearsed earlier. Her chest flushes, peppering pink across her tits. The color tells on her, that she's intimidated and turned on by me. It's probably the damn paint. Tyra made my face appear sinister, just the way I like it. I'm a fucked-up bastard because it only makes my cock harder, and right now is the perfect time to show it off. "Please! Someone help. I can't go to the dark side."

I grab her ankle, giving it a swift tug. She yells again. It's all part of the show we'd come up with. Saint flips the stereo on, 'Descent' by Fear Factory pulsing low throughout the room.

"You won't be going anywhere," I thunder out the promise, shifting her small frame back until she's propped on all fours in front of me. She's had angel wings airbrushed on her back, and I have to admit, they'd look awesome tatted permanently. I give her ass a firm squeeze, enjoying her sweet whimper under my touch, and then put the condom to my lips. I tear the package with my teeth and free the rubber. Sheathing my length, I lean over to bite up her back along the sensitive flesh and tug her hair harshly. My stance widens so the camera can get a good view of everything happening, pausing momentarily for Ruin to zero in on her puckered asshole. It sells and that's what matters. Besides, it's a sexy-as-fuck part on a woman, regardless.

My fingers find her opening, making sure her pussy's relaxed and wet enough for me to slide right in. The last thing I want to do is hurt her in any of this. That's one thing I've learned in this process: if the chick doesn't trust me even a little bit, then it won't work.

"Soaked!" I exclaim. "You want this! You're already a sinner!" I roar and plunge inside her. She moans loudly, and I concentrate on her firm body, along with the way her cunt squeezes my cock.

Clenching my eyes closed, I imagine sinking into the forbidden Leigh. I know her pussy has to be the best there is, and the knowledge haunts me, along with the thought of anyone else touching her that way.

"Ah!" Bambi exclaims a bit shriller than her typical porn voice, and I part my eyelids, taking the situation in. My hands clenched around her hip tight enough to leave behind bruises, and it hits me that I was going too hard on her with my thoughts taking a sharp turn south. Maybe picturing my fantasy woman in front of me on all fours, ready for my cock, isn't the smartest thing right now, but when will it ever be?

She's forbidden. My best friend's younger sister. The princess of the club. I'd die if I ever touched her. The Kings of Carnage would make sure of it.

I give the audience what they want, what they pay for. I fuck Bambi long and hard, just enough to satisfy our biggest customers. I'm frustrated with Leigh, so goddamn wound up from having to keep my distance and not go after what I truly desire, that I take a bit of it out on Bambi. It makes for good footage, and in this business, the kinkier the better.

I'm not tied down to anyone. I belong to no one. Technically, not even to the club at this point. I'm only a prospect, and yet, the chick I crave is dangling just too far out in front of me. I can reach all I want, but it'll never happen. The sooner I can make peace with it, the better, I suppose. Coming to terms with never having Leigh in my future leaves a sour taste in my mouth, no matter how I think of it. I was fine until she stepped foot in my bedroom not wearing any clothes. Then it was like a switch was flipped inside me, and suddenly she's all I can see now.

"Fuck," I mutter to myself, ripping the condom off my length and tossing it in the toilet. I flush it, wash my dick and my hands, then make my way back into the room to get dressed. I'll take a shower at my place with my own shit. Some wash here, but I prefer my personal space.

"You good?" Ruin approaches, concern in his gaze.

I release a breath and nod. "Yeah, man, I'm straight. What's up?" I grab for my pants and tug them on.

"You seemed different today. Was it Leigh? Did she say something outside?"

I trek my hands through my hair, then reach for my cut. Sliding the leather on, I push my feet in my boots. "She said nothing. It was weird, like she was mad at me for some reason. Don't have a clue what I did." I attempt to shrug it off, but it doesn't work. Her being upset doesn't feel right to me, and everything in me wants to fix it, to find her and make sure she's okay.

"It's my sister, Spade." He calls me by my last name. We've done it since we were young. We'd always talked about it being my road name someday, but we got older and realized it was a dumb move to have my last name advertised on my cut. "There's no telling what she's got going on in her head. She's probably still upset over her dog."

I nod, although I don't completely agree. "Right. I'm sure that's it."

"Next time you see her, it'll be same as always," he assures me and I nod again, beginning to feel a little better about her leaving like she did. "Stop by the shop later if you're out. I have to ink a new guy working down at Jupiter's garage."

"All right, man, I'm out. Gonna take a shower and chill. I'll catch you at the club later if I don't hit up the tattoo shop."

"Yeah, bro, ride safe." He fist bumps me and I say my good-byes to everyone else.

The ride does me some good, getting me feeling back to normal. One thing's still gnawing at the back of my mind, however. Leigh.

I seriously cannot wait until all the pieces come together and I finally understand why I went through everything I did.
- Word Porn

Leigh

Stupid motherfucking fuck-fuck! That's exactly the way I feel about Sterling in that damn porn house. I have absolutely no right to feel any way about it, yet of course I do. I've known him my entire life. How many people can you honestly say that about? Regardless, that fact alone gives me no right whatsoever to be angry over what he's doing at the moment. He's not mine. He belongs to no one, a fact he's made well-known around town. Not that my father would ever go for me and Sterling together or anything, but still, the thought has crossed my mind a time or two.

Okay, that's a lie. I've been silently crushing on my brother's best friend for as long as I can remember. Sterling has always stood up for me like my own brother, yet he's never looked brotherly to me. He's always been a little bit beautiful in my eyes. His manwhorish ways in high school helped stomp my heart out for him a bit for years, but now that I've gotten older, things have changed. My feelings for him have evolved from a small-time crush to obsessive, to heartbroken, to something else entirely. I'm at the stage where I crave him, no matter what parts I'll get or how much. I deserve more, I'm acutely aware, but when you care for someone, you're willing to accept whatever may be offered. In this case, if Sterling were to only offer up his dick, well, I'd hop on it.

I want to know he's in my bed, filling me up, rather than some stupid porn slut. Unfortunately for me, I haven't figured out just how to accomplish that feat. I thought for sure me staying over at his place, in his bed, would've sparked something between us. In a way, I feel like it did...but it wasn't enough of a push for him. Granted, I was wrecked over Duke and his horrific death right before my eyes, but it was the perfect opportunity for Sterling to comfort me and for our feelings to bloom. I say *our feelings,* because deep down he has to feel some type of a way about me in return. There's no way you can care for someone this long, love them even, and they not have some sort of sexual affections for you in return.

I have to make him start noticing me in a different light, but the manner is the real kicker. I have no idea how to get the man's attention in a sexual aspect. I mean, he does porn for a living and has women throwing themselves at him left and right. Besides, that's not the type of woman I am, so I'd probably suck at it. I need to figure out how to be provocative in his eyes.

I end up at my parents', close to the club, wanting to go sit by Duke and talk to him. He was the best freaking dog. I'd had him since I turned thirteen. Dad was adamant of me having some sort of protector by my side at all times. He has a hard time trusting men around me who aren't my brother, Bash, Sterling, and Stryker. The answer to him was Duke coming into my life. My parents had him specially trained. He was bred to be a K-9 officer, but I got him instead. He lived a good doggy life. I fed him lots of treats over the years and played fetch with him until my arm grew tired more times than I can count, and yet he remained true. He was by my side to help me through everything, whether it was a broken heart or a sketchy guy eyeing me up while I walked. He was my best friend and will forever hold a place in my heart.

I pat the dirt, murmuring that I wish he were still alive but he'll always be with me. I'm interrupted by footsteps approaching. "Hey," I call, already knowing it's Mom. Ruin's busy making porn with Sterling and my dad's always at the club during the day. He's there a lot of nights as well, usually with Mom by his side. I can't blame him. We're older now, and all of their friends hang out there.

"Hey, pretty girl. How are you today?" she greets, moving to sit at my side. Her arm wraps around my back, coming to rest on my opposite shoulder. We're a lot alike, me and her. It's been a blessing and a curse. If I'm having a tough time, she knows how to comfort me, but if I'm pissed or hiding something, she can usually read me like a book.

"Just missing him," I share, not wanting to confess everything else on my mind. I wish I could open up to her about the feelings I've harbored for Sterling over the years and what I just saw. Maybe ask for some advice in that department, but I can't. I know she'd speak to Dad about it, and I don't want him to hurt Sterling. Not that I blame her for telling Dad everything. It's just the way they are with each other.

"You should take your dad up on his offer for another. He won't be replacing Duke, but he'll be there for you to lean on in the very least."

"I'm not ready. It's too soon. I don't know if I'll ever get another dog."

"Please don't say that. I worry about you, especially now that you live alone. I felt better knowing Duke was beside you every night, but now you're all alone. It's unsettling. Trust me when I say you never know who's around, who could be watching you without you realizing it." Her gaze is full of worry, but she needn't be so consumed by her thoughts. I'm an adult and a strong one at that.

"I'm safe," I promise her.

"I know you are, but I'm your mom. It's my job to worry. How about you stay here for a while? You won't be alone so much with one of us always around. It might be nice being close to your parents while you get through this."

"I love you both, but I'll be okay. Ruin texted me and they got the guy who hit Duke."

She nods. "I heard. Sterling should've waited for your father before going after him, but what can I expect? That boy is family."

A surprised gasp leaves me before I can hold it back. My heart beats double-time. I'm here mourning, and yet this news now has my thoughts elsewhere. "Sterling?" I ask again, needing to clarify I wasn't imagining her saying his name. My brother told me they caught the bastard and he would never come near me again but conveniently left out the details it appears.

Her head bobs, her arms falling from my shoulder to wrap around her legs. She draws them close and lays the side of her head on them as she watches me. "Yes, it was Sterling. You didn't know?"

My nose screws up as I shake my head. "Please tell me."

She sighs. "I'm probably not supposed to since you don't already know, but it directly involves you, and you're an adult now. I don't know much, but I can tell you what your father shared with me. I'd been hounding him, otherwise he'd never have said anything."

I nod, waiting for any small morsel of information she'll offer up. My mind is racing at the moment with discovering Sterling was the one who went to stand up for me. I'll be forever grateful, no matter how jealous I get knowing he's with other women doing porn. It feels good knowing he has my back as well.

"So, from what Dad told me, you left Sterling's place to come here. Sterling texted Ruin letting him know that he was going after the guy who killed Duke. Your brother told Dad, of course, so him and a few of the guys went after Sterling. They didn't want him potentially getting shot, and they wanted to confront the person who threatened you themselves."

"He didn't threaten me, though. Just my dog."

She disagrees, her brows skyrocketing. "Of course he did! What he pulled was a direct threat to the club's princess, and he should've known your father would never stand for such disrespect."

I don't want to go into it any further so I ask, "What else happened?"

"Sterling had the other kid out in the middle of his lawn, beating the pulp out of him," she admits with a small grin.

My eyes widen. "Did the law show up? Sterling didn't get in trouble, did he?" He did that...for me? I can't help but feel warm all over, knowing he went after Bruce. Not because he hurt him or anything, but because he could've stepped aside and let my brother or father handle it, but he didn't. He chose to stand up for me himself. It has to mean *something,* right?

"Of course not. You know how Bash is about keeping that boy away from the law." She says it as if we're talking about a teenage troublemaker and not a twenty-two-year-old man prospecting for the club who doesn't have a rap sheet.

I bob my head, wanting more deets. "He's okay, right? Sterling, I mean."

"Yes. Probably upset the club showed up to ruin his fun, but he shouldn't have pulled that without consulting your father first. Regardless, he pointed out the problem, and Dad was able to make sure you'd be safe in the future. And, yes, Sterling did that for you. He'd do whatever he had to, to protect you. He's been that way for as long as I can remember."

My lips tilt into a smile. Hearing her say it makes it real. I wish he would've said something when I saw him earlier. There wasn't a mark on him—I'd have noticed—so Bruce must've not gotten a chance with Sterling coming at him. I wish I could've seen it. I don't generally seek out fights to watch, but that would've been one I'd have paid money to witness.

"Thanks for telling me. See? There's no real reason for you to worry. I've got my protectors if I need something."

"Thank God," I manage to catch her muttering under her breath before she stands, holding her hand out to me.

I say nothing about it, as I don't think I was supposed to hear her comment. I place my palm in hers, and she helps tug me up. She asks, "Are you going to be okay going into work today? I came over to make sure and let you know what time it is."

Nodding, I offer her a hug and say, "Yes. I'm feeling a bit better having come out here. I needed time to decompress and think."

"Hey, I'm not complaining, quite the opposite. I'll keep ya here as long as you'll allow it." She offers me a wide smile, and I can't help but return it. She really has been the best mom to me. So many people I know ended up fucked up, and I'm grateful I'm not one of them. I'm sure people out there would argue, being that I grew up around an MC, but they have no idea what they'd be talking about.

"I'll be back for Sunday dinner, promise," I say as we stop beside my driver's side door.

"I better see you before then."

"You will." I pop a quick peck on her cheek. "Love ya, Mom."

"I love you. Drive safely."

I nod as I climb into the small Honda Civic. Backing out of the driveway, Billy Idol's 'Rebel Yell' comes on the classic rock station, and the song has me belting out the lyrics as I head for my apartment. The music, along with thoughts of Sterling beating up Bruce for me, is enough to consume my thoughts for the ride.

"Your brother and Sterling are here," Shauna, the other employee, informs me as I finish taking money from a customer.

I tell the person waiting on their smoothies, "It'll be right out, thank you." I slide the drive-thru window closed and spin around. "Did they ask for me, or are you just letting me know?"

"They ordered, but asked if you'd make their drinks."

"Okay," I easily concede. "Want to switch with me?" I gesture to the window and she nods, heading to the other blender area. The shop isn't too big, but it's large enough for us to have two bars full of smoothie ingredients, along with a wall of flavors for snow cones. It's nothing grand, but I've worked here since I was sixteen and I enjoy it. The customers are used to me and are friendly enough.

I don't need to see the ticket to know what they've ordered. My brother only gets one thing: the banana pudding smoothie with protein. Sterling gocs for the Oasis which has strawberry, coconut, and orange. I like that one too. Go figure. I grab the drinks and make my way to one of the five booths the shops has. They're sprawled out over each side like they own the place. "Hey," I mutter, setting the smoothies before them.

"Sterling said you were weird when you left the studio," Ruin begins, not one to beat around the bush.

"That was three days ago," I remind, glancing at each of them as I sit in the spot next to my brother. I attempt not to linger too long on Sterling, but I can't help it. He has an alluring presence. It's always been that way where he's concerned. "I've been too busy working every day to stop back by or worry about what y'all have been getting up to," I toss in for good measure.

Sterling grunts, taking a long draw from his straw.

"You should start bartending. You'd make so much more money," Ruin comments. He always says the same thing.

I reply in tandem, "I love my job and Dad would lose his shit. You know it as well as I do."

He scoffs. "I have a porn business. Doubt you can do any wrong in his eyes. No matter what it is, let alone bartending. It's what you do now, only for adults."

I grow quiet as he brings up his business. Don't get me wrong, porn itself doesn't bother me, neither does Ruin filming it, or possibly being in the videos himself. The only thing that grinds on me is knowing Sterling is doing it with other women. If he wants to record himself fucking, then at least let me be in it with him. "Did you come here to lecture me, or was there another reason?"

Sterling finally says, "Your mom wanted us to remind you about family dinner."

I roll my eyes. "So, in other words, she sent you guys to check on me. When will all of you realize that I'm fine? I'll ask for help if

I need it!" I declare, exasperated.

Sterling's palms shoot up, his gaze taking me in and warming a few degrees. "Hey, I know you're a capable woman, believe me."

Ruin shoots him a glare. "Bro, shut the fuck up."

I can't help but grin at the sudden glowering going on between the two of them. I know nothing will come of it. They've gotten pissed in the past at each other and it never lasts long. One always gives in to admit they were wrong and their friendship goes back to normal as if the hiccup never existed.

"Tell her I'm fine. Where's Tyra, anyhow?" I bring up his chick to change the subject.

"With Poe. She was gonna do a few piercings and stuff for him."

I nod and tease, "Must've gotten sick of you wanting her to call you daddy."

Sterling chuckles while Ruin rolls his eyes, ignoring the dig. "She'll be around later."

"What about you, Ster?" I can't help but ask.

"I won't complain if you call me daddy, but Ruin may be uncomfortable," he flirts.

"Does that ever work?" I ask.

"You'd be surprised what names I can get out of a chick's mouth," he retorts, and I'm back to being pissed off again.

I stand up, determined not to huff and make them aware I'm angry. "I'm out of breaks. I'll see you guys later."

Sterling's face twists in confusion as my brother says bye without a second thought, then follows suit. I head back to the counter area to let Shauna know I can get back to the drive-thru. I don't know why I've been getting emotional around Sterling lately. It's definitely gotten worse. I was never this bad. I've seen my fair share of women with him. Even if they were splashed across his body like a leech and sucking face, it never made me angry in the past. Now, however, I'm positively fuming inside.

I throw myself into helping customers and cleaning anything I get a chance to. It helps my night go by quickly, and I know the owner will be pleased with the way everything looks. Working a smoothie shop may not be everyone's dream job, but I happen to love it. I have fun mixing up new flavors and I've gotten fairly good at it. The owner has let me take over the specials, and once a month I come up with a new combination to offer customers. They've been a hit and we've gotten lots of requests for those recipes, even after the specials are over and we have new combinations. Someday, I hope to either take over this place completely or open up my own shop. Maybe sell some cool merchandise along with specialty drinks or something of that nature to bring it to the next level.

My friend Magnolia texts me, inviting me out. We haven't been as close lately like we used to be. She opted for college, whereas I decided to work more hours. I figure I can go to college when I'm ready, if I'm ever ready, that is. People glorify getting rich and having special titles far too much, in my opinion. Family and happiness are the most important things in my mind, and college doesn't seem to fit into those priorities right now. Not that the other route is wrong or anything. I mean my mom went to college and graduated, as did my aunt, and Savannah, Sterling's mom.

I text her back that I'm too tired tonight, but maybe another night. Lord knows I need to do something to get Sterling off my mind. A night out couldn't hurt, along with a hot guy or two to play with. I don't even attempt to find a guy to replace Sterling anymore. I know it'll most likely never happen. But that doesn't mean I can't have some fun until the stubborn prospect wakes up and finally realizes I've been waiting for him.

I head home, managing to spook myself in the parking lot. I'm not completely used to Duke not being by my side and it's had me a bit on edge. Not to mention, I miss him more than what people probably consider normal. I get inside my apartment, lock the door, and pull my phone out again. No matter how many times I check it, there's never a message from Sterling.

I'm home. Love you guys.

I send the text to our family's group chat. I know they worry, and instead of allowing it to annoy me, I give them the small piece of mind with a text. I send another off to Sterling, telling him I'll be partying with Magnolia tomorrow and to stop by if he wants. He won't, but one day, I hope he will.

My mission in life is not merely to survive, but to thrive; and to do so with some passion, some compassion, some humor, and some style.

\- Maya Angelou

Sterling

"You free for this next run?" Dad asks, and I nod immediately. The club and my prospecting duties come first at this point in my life. They probably always will, my future included. I want my patch so badly I can practically taste it. I've been a grunt for the club for too long already, tired of doing the dirty work of washing bikes and running errands. I'm ready to be a brother and receive the respect that comes along with that patch.

"Of course. Anything you need. When will we ride out?"

With another run under my belt, it'll be another step closer to getting my hard-earned spot. I've never wanted something so badly in my life. Get voted into the Kings of Carnage MC and work alongside my father amongst everyone else I've been surrounded by my entire life. They're my family away from my immediate family and I couldn't imagine taking a different path. What Chaos and my dad pay me for the runs are pennies compared to the payout I'll receive once I wear a member patch. Hell, most prospects don't get a cut at all, but I'm risking my life for this club every single time I'm either driving or following our gun shipments, and they recognize as much.

"Few days, waiting on one last transaction to come through," he grumbles, grabbing two beers from a club slut. He hands one to me and we both twist off the caps, taking a deep pull from the chilled beverage. "Your mom was taking Sawyer to get her license today," he eventually says, and my mouth drops. It explains his gruff demeanor today. I thought he may've been pissed at me over something I'd done, but I guess this is the true culprit.

"Why?"

"Cause she's sixteen. Lord fuckin' help me."

"But Stryker can take her wherever she needs to go," I argue, not ready for my baby sister to have that freedom without a bit of protection from one of us.

"Trust me, I said the same damn thing."

"And?"

"Your momma wasn't having it. Thought the woman was gonna twist my balls and serve them to me on a platter for even mentioning we wait on Sawyer getting her license."

"Sawyer's so...innocent. How can we protect her if she's not around one of us?" I finally ask. My sister is smart and quick-witted, but she's a huge nerd. I don't mean that in a negative sense. It's just the truth. If one of the club's enemies went after her, she wouldn't stand a chance, and I can't imagine a world that doesn't have Sawyer in it. She's special...to all of us.

He shakes his head. "Gonna stroke out over the shit if I don't let it go and have confidence in my girl." He takes a hefty swig of the beer and it has me thinking the old man will be doing shots before the day is over. Mom will have to come pick his ass up, no doubt. Not that she minds. My parents love taking care of each other and never hesitate to go out of their way for each other.

"I understand that. Sawyer's intelligent, but Dad, she's so tiny."

He blows out a heavy breath, shooting me a glare, and digs his smokes free. "I fucking know it. I'm still trying to come up with something."

"You have ideas?"

He nods, placing the cigarette between his lips and lighting it up. He's never been a heavy smoker. Only when he's stressing about something. "Thinking about putting a tracker under her car."

"Hell yeah, I say we do it. Maybe find another to toss in her shoes or something. We can have her location pegged twenty-four hours a day."

He snorts. "Have you seen how many pairs of shoes she owns? That'd be half her damn closet. Think, son. She may not have her phone on her all the time. Otherwise, I'd just keep up with her that way and not worry about a backup plan."

"What about putting one in a necklace?" She doesn't have a lot of jewelry, so if it were something dainty but nice, she'd probably never take it off.

His eyes sparkle as he exhales smoke in the opposite direction of me. "Now we're talking." He drums his fingers, thinking aloud. "It'd have to be waterproof. I wonder who makes something like that around here. I wonder if there's a spot in Atlanta that could pull it off without Sawyer being tipped about it?"

I shrug. "Probably. I'd at least check into it. Ask Mom. She'd know."

He mutters, "Not sure I should mention it. She may rip me a new one. You know how independent she is, and she expects it from Sawyer too. I don't think my girl's got that bit of wild in her that your momma does though."

"You're being protective. Mom can appreciate as much. She'll probably be on board with it. Don't be surprised if she's suspect in the future if you give her jewelry though."

He chuckles. "No shit." Then nods, "You're right. And if you're not, then it'll be up to you to follow Sawyer around town."

I huff. Forever the oldest. I wouldn't trade it though. My siblings may be pain in the asses at times, but they're my family and I love them. "A prospect riding at her back all the time, yeah, she'd be thrilled with that one. You wouldn't just have Mom on you. It'd be Sawyer as well. Have fun with that."

He shrugs. "I'll always do what I have to, to protect my girls. You and Stryker are too damn stubborn. Never had to worry about you assholes."

I laugh, 'cause it's true. "Glad I don't have any kids to worry about."

His brows jump. "Someday, just watch. A woman will come along when you're least expecting it. She'll knock you on your ass, and then all you'll be able to see is her and your future."

"Well, if that ever happens...I still have plenty of time to go before then. I'm focusing on the club and Porn Kings. Everything else can come down the road," I reply adamantly, with Leigh's face popping into the back of my mind.

He grunts. His gaze is full of something I don't want to ask about. I don't care what he may know through his experience that I don't. I meant what I said. I have plenty of time before I have to worry about anything or anyone new coming along and settling down.

Chaos approaches, grabbing his own beer, Ruin and Jinx at his side. "Everything good over here?" he asks.

My dad replies, "Yep, just filling Sterling in on the newest Sawyer development. Kid's helping me come up with ideas."

Chaos chuckles. "I told you, shit wasn't fun for me when I was going through it with Leigh. I fucking lucked out, being she's such a good driver and I could keep up with her driving speed on our insurance app. I'd never tell her as much though. I want that girl staying vigilant."

Jinx says, "With Ruin and Sterling, they'd been riding dirt bikes since they were this tall." He holds his hand waist-high. I've heard this story several times. "Little shits belonged on a bike. It's in their blood. Never have to worry about them fucking off, and at least we're only stuck looking at a few of their ugly mugs and not all of them," he razzes me and Ruin while our fathers chuckle and agree. They've always been this way, easygoing and giving us shit. It's how you know they care. If they didn't, they wouldn't acknowledge us. The men around here are a bunch of stubborn old asses, but they've seen some shit in their time together, so I can't blame them for it.

Sly approaches, tucking his cell away. "Glad I caught you guys together, that old bike and auto shop down by the pub was hit hard when the last club rolled through. I've been getting a few calls from the girls at Centerfolds about shit they've overheard."

"Fuck," Chaos grates, and we all dip our heads in agreement.

It hits me what's beside the pub and I ask, "Wait, Jupiter's business?" We all know the place, having had to stop by from time to time. The old owner's daughter took it over and she's never been one to snub us. This doesn't sit well with me, she didn't deserve any blowback from club shit. I need to stop in and have my tires aligned.

It'll give me the perfect opportunity to check out the damage and make sure she's straight. She's young too. This certainly can't be easy on her.

Dad murmurs, "Doesn't look good on the club, and we've finally made a name for ourselves here. It's taken long enough. I don't want any old ghosts or rumors to come crawling back."

Jinx leans in, quietly saying, "We don't need any law enforcement poking their head into our shit either." He flicks his gaze to Dad, and Dad's jaw hardens. Cops are bad for business when you run guns, amongst other things, for the club. He and Jinx used to be heavy into selling drugs, but Dad gave it up at the prospect of only selling guns instead. One thing I learned at a young age is we don't judge around here. You mind your fucking business unless asked otherwise, and I've made it my mission to do as much.

Sly mutters, "No one will come to the club for help. They'll be too afraid to ask, no matter how long we've been around. Hell, we damn near own half the town by now and still they're too frightened. If it weren't for Centerfolds, we wouldn't know half of what we do. I wonder if North knows anymore."

"We need to figure out something to get their minds off everything," Chaos declares. "I'll bring it up a few times around different folks and see what they have to say on the matter. Maybe a few of the other prospects know something."

Ruin glances to me and doesn't have to say a word. I know exactly what he's thinking. We just bought a bunch of new equipment for the studio and there's no way we can come out of pocket in good faith to help other people without us feeling it hit our pockets. We make decent money, but we also invest it.

I raise my brows, letting him know that I get it and feel the same way. Hopefully, whatever Chaos comes up with won't anticipate us having to pitch in. Sounds fucked up, but we're young and don't have a lot of chances to build our personal investments up. It takes time, I'm discovering.

"How's Leigh doing? She getting through everything all right?" Dad speaks up, asking the same thing I've been wondering. "Things still calm and quiet for her?"

"It is," Chaos admits. "Not sure if I should be relieved or worried." He pins his gaze on Ruin. "You check in with her today?"

"Yep and we dropped by her job yesterday. Sat for a few. Me and Spade have been making sure she's safe." He chin lifts in my direction

"Good, keep it up. I'll see you later," he replies then addresses the rest of us. "I'm headed to the house for a bit. See what you can find out about businesses hit from that fucking club."

I take his cue and leave as well. I need some space from everyone before tomorrow night. Leigh has had my head twisted up a bit since she showed up on my doorstep. I can't afford to be distracted. Dad could call on me at any time for that run, and I refuse to be a liability to the club because I don't have my mind right.

I silently lecture myself the entire ride home, even while I swing by Leigh's job to see her car parked out front. I don't stop, but I still manage to go out of my way to find out where she's at. She's safe. That's all I need to know before I head in the opposite direction and find my bed.

"I'm glad you could make it," Cambri greets with a warm smile as I make my way into the oversized grassy backyard right by the club. They've lived here my entire life, so it's always felt like a third home.

I say third because of my parents' place, the club, and then here.

"You know I'm not missing it if you're cooking," I tease, and she swats my arm.

"You guys and your endless stomachs." She rolls her eyes, but I'm used to it. I'm practically her adopted child. Me and Ruin have been glued to each other's sides for so long.

"Ruin not here yet?" I ask, wondering why his bike wasn't out front. He's usually the first to arrive if we're not together. Things have been a little different with Tyra, but I respect his time with her. She means a lot to him now and is cool as fuck, so I'm happy they've found each other.

She shakes her head. "No, I sent him and Tyra to the store. They'll be here soon."

"I would've stopped," I offer.

"I know, but I wanted a minute with you anyway."

My brows jump, and I stand a bit straighter. She doesn't usually say anything to me unless it's to have me warn off someone from Leigh, and that hasn't happened since she got out of school. "Should I be worried? I can get Stryker to back me up if someone's bothering Leigh."

She grins. "No. I wanted to thank you for what you did for Leigh though. You've always been there in the shadows for her, and while she may not know it, I do. You've been her silent protector. You've helped put my mind at ease many times. I told her about you standing up for her last week. I worry about her, and you deserve to finally get some credit, Sterling."

"I didn't do anything Ruin or Chaos wouldn't have done. I don't need any acknowledgment. Seriously, I just want her taken care of."

She squeezes my arm. "I know. You're a good man. You remind

me so much of Bash, especially when I first met him. He's always been so loyal and protective of your mom and you kids. You'll make a good provider someday."

I nod, taking her words as the compliment they are. Dad's always been fiercely steadfast and defensive whenever it comes to people he cares about, and that extends to the club and his brothers. "Is she angry about it?" I eventually ask. It's the reason I never told Leigh I was going after Bruce in the first place. She was already torn up over losing Duke. I didn't want to add any more turmoil to her load.

She laughs. "On the contrary, I think she was a little flattered." I can feel my face heat with her admission, which is a strange reaction for me. "Will you grab the pitcher of tea from the fridge? It's too nice of a day to waste eating inside." I'm grateful for her changing the subject and offering me an out from discussing how Leigh feels about me.

"Of course," I agree and move for the back door. As I enter the kitchen I can feel her presence...Leigh stands there, ass propped against the counter in front of the sink. She's looking straight at me. Could she have been watching out the window? Did she know I was coming inside?

"Sup, Boo." I flash my gaze over her briefly and move to the refrigerator. Opening the door, I bask in the cool air. The small glimpse at Leigh was enough to have my chest tightening. She's sexy as fuck in a little sundress that manages to show off her curves. She looks like she spent the day outside, sunbathing, just to accomplish that perfect sun-kissed complexion of hers.

"Mom forgot the watermelon, so Ruin's picking one up," she responds rather than returning my greeting. I'm usually digging into the watermelon when I'm here, and Cambri's gotten in the habit of having some if she knows I'll be around. My mom's the same way with Ruin, always having stuff he enjoys at the house if he stops by.

"I'm here for the tea."

"Oh."

I turn around, setting it on the counter before moving beside her for a cup. My arm brushes hers, my nerves on high alert. She draws in a quick breath, but I can't concentrate on it when her scent manages to surround me at the same moment. I don't know what it is, or how to describe it, but it damn near puts my mind in a daze. "Leigh, I—"

"Sterling—"

We both say at the same time, and my eyes drop to her mouth. Her lips are perfect, plump enough they make me crave her kiss, even though I know I shouldn't. I reach up, my hand moving to cup her cheek.

"Boo—" I murmur, wanting so badly to lean in and kiss her. I need to touch her, pull her curvy body to mine and feel her warmness against my chest like I had the night she slept in my bed. She was so fucking perfect and she hadn't realized it. Even being a mess over her dog, I couldn't get over how grown up and beautiful she's suddenly become in my eyes.

The pads of my fingers barely manage to touch her silky skin when we're interrupted by Ruin calling out that he's returned from the store. I jolt away, moving to grab the cup I'd intended to get and use it to put some ice in the pitcher of tea. "Anybody inside?" Ruin hollers again.

I yell back, "Yeah. We're in here, man."

He finds us in the kitchen, carting a massive watermelon along with him and Tyra. It's damn near the size of a fucking car tire, so on the upside, I'll get to take some home with me for later. His stare pings between me and Leigh, his expression growing curious. "Everything okay in here?" The air is tense, I can taste the thickness on my tongue.

I chin lift to Tyra, not wanting to be a dick and not acknowledge her.

Leigh sighs. "Just peachy, Ruin. Come on, Tyra, let's see if Mom needs anything else." They take off out the back door while Ruin grabs a massive knife.

He begins to carve up my favorite fruit, making a mess all over the counter. I grab a bowl for him, setting it beside the slices. "She still pissed at us for checking in on her the other day?" he eventually asks.

"Bro, you're asking the wrong person. That's your sister, not mine." That fact has never stood out to me more than now. I may've considered her a sister type in my past, but then we grew up and she straight out glowed up. Bitch is hot enough she'd have any guy doing a double-take plus more. Just the thought of her coming around with a man eventually has me feeling salty, when I don't have any right to be.

"Chicks are confusing," he eventually comments.

I nod. "The fuck are we going to do if your dad has us pitch in for the town? Has he said anything yet?"

He shrugs. "The club already gets half our profit from Porn Kings. Sales have been picking up a lot, so I doubt he asks us for anything. He knows we've been doing our part and holding up our end."

"I'm just trying to bank what I can. Who knows how long I have before I eventually get popped by the cops, and I want to make sure I can afford one helluva attorney if I need it. You feel me?"

"Yeah, I get it, and Bash has your back. He's telling you to do the right thing and save up some of your cash. If I were moving guns all the time, I'd be doing the same."

I nod, agreeing with him. Dad wouldn't tell me to put some money away if it wasn't for something important, and if it's not to bail my ass out of jail someday, then it's for the family he thinks I'll have eventually. He wasn't into guns when he met Mom, so he doesn't realize how hard the gun business can be when looking for a potential forever prospect. I don't want to fall for someone then be forced to lie to her for the rest of my life. It's why I need to stay focused and concentrate on the club, not some mystical forever pussy he talks about.

Ruin hands me a bowl full of sliced fruit and grabs another, filling it with the leftover pieces. "Let's get this outside before Mom comes looking for us. Or worse, Leigh decides to tell Tyra shit from my past."

I chuckle, following him outside with the tea and bowl. Leigh has always stirred up shit when Ruin liked someone. I found it amusing, but stayed out of it. Luckily, Sawyer is young enough she never got to pull that shit with me. There's a six-year age gap between us, so we've always been in different levels of life, unlike her and Stryker. Those two went through most of school together, being two years a part. My brother did a good job making sure Sawyer was protected. Now, she's alone until she graduates, and it has me wanting to pull into the high school parking lot every day, just to show the little assholes she still has someone at her back.

"Fuck," he mutters the curse, reminding me of Chaos. "Tyra's glaring and Leigh's smiling. I'm fucked."

I can't help but laugh. I love seeing Leigh's face light up with mischief. If I were smart, that thought alone would fucking terrify me.

You'll never leave where you are until y
ou decide where you'd rather be.
- Pinterest Meme

Leigh

"We need to raise some money, do something to help Jupiter's Bike and Auto Shop out," my father rumbles from his seat. I hear him and Mom discuss it for a few with my uncle Poe and Bash. They toy around with doing a club donation or an actual fundraiser. They've done several in the past, always trying to help someone out. If only people knew how much good they do, but Dad's stubborn and does a lot of things anonymously. I think it's how you know he has a good heart—he doesn't do it for recognition, but because he genuinely cares.

My mom's always stood right beside him through it all too. She's just as passionate about these things as he can be, and sometimes more, depending on what it is. The sex trade, for example. My mom is crazy when it comes to helping stop the horrible sex trafficking business going on in the world. I think if she could go out and save every woman affected by it, she would. It's just the kind of person she is.

I'm definitely not on her level yet, but I do try to help whenever I can. I think it's particularly important to be willing to go out of my way for someone in true need. I believe in karma, and you never know when you may need that help and support in return. I rack my brain, thinking of what is easy enough, people will volunteer their time and we'll be able to collect a decent amount of money to get Jupiter what she may need. I saw her front window was cracked when I drove by—probably by a stray bullet or something. I know she most likely has more damage we can't easily see.

"How about a car wash?" I toss out, not expecting them to take my suggestion seriously. I learned long ago that unless someone asks for your opinion, they typically don't care what it is. I take a sip from my Dr. Pepper and catalog Sterling's location. It's probably the twentieth time I've done it since arriving at the clubhouse. At this point, I can tell you where he's at, what he's doing, and what he's wearing. I need to chill out with this crap. The man is not a freaking lollipop waiting for my long lost lick.

Dad's face brightens, offering me a pleased grin, and Bash bobs his head as well. "Hell, why not?"

"We could have it down at Mooney's," Sly suggests, finally breaking his silence. "I can run some numbers and possibly get some drink specials going on at the pub. Maybe make the difference as part of the donation." He nods to himself saying, "This could really work out."

"It's simple and costs next to nothing," Mom easily agrees. She's good about having my back when it comes to my ideas. Girl code and all that. We have to stick together in a room full of burly bikers who like to get their way. Although, I hope it's also because I come up with decent suggestions and not only because I'm her daughter.

"Stryker will help wherever you need him to. He needs as much good karma as possible with how many assholes he's pissed off around town," Bash mutters, and my father flashes him a grin. Those two have been close since before I was born, part of the reason why I refer to Bash and Poe as my adopted uncles. The entire club has always been my extended family. 'Uncle' Bash taught me how to play pool so I could try to swindle my father out of a bet when I was twelve. It almost worked until Dad caught Bash mouthing at me about what to do. Dad was a good sport about it, but he doesn't bet while playing pool with me anymore.

"I'll help with whatever I can," I offer, always willing to pitch in for the club when allowed. I learned early on not to overstep where Dad's club is concerned. Sure they're extended family, but it's also his business, and being the president, the bulk of decisions fall to him. I don't know how he does it. Some of the stuff I've heard the club has gone through is crazy. I've never been told much of anything outright, but I've caught bits and pieces over the years. It's best if I keep my nose out of it and enjoy the good that comes from it, like Sterling sans shirt in a leather cut and jeans. The man is a walking tease to the female population, and half the time he's oblivious to it.

"I can get with Savannah and we can bake some stuff too. I know she'll want to help," Mom suggests, and Dad immediately picks up on it. If he has her support on something then he almost always goes for it.

Jupiter is close to my age, so I'm sure this has to be overwhelming for her. With the club offering their help, hopefully she sees it for the blessing it is and doesn't get too frightened with their attention. Maybe if I'm the one who talks to her about it, she won't. I'll catch Dad by himself and suggest it, that way it'll seem like his idea to everyone else and he'll agree. Mom has taught me that, with the right approach, men can be too easy to offer what you want. You just have to know how to ask for it. Too bad that doesn't seem to apply to Sterling in my case. The man has missed every signal I've sent him over the years. The next step would be setting off fireworks and Dad would be pissed.

"Then it's settled. We'll make it happen."

AND THAT'S EXACTLY HOW I GOT ROPED INTO HELPING PLAN THE CLUB'S fundraiser for Jupiter. It wasn't hard or anything, and I got to be involved with them and their families. Being around everyone always makes me feel good. I couldn't imagine living another type of life than the one I've been given. Jupiter is sweet too. She was a bit stunned to find out the club was planning to help her without any type of strings attached. I can understand her being leery. There're clubs out there like the one that came into town and messed her shop up. If they were the bikers I knew, I'd be keeping my distance as well, but Kings of Carnage aren't evil. Don't get me wrong, Dad's a total badass, I've seen him and Bash punch a few guys before, and it was the most exciting thing ever. I shouldn't get enthusiastic over it, but I did, and I'll never forget it. Besides, those jerks deserved it.

There's also the detail that Sterling has stopped by Jupiter's shop a few times. In the beginning, I guess it was for some car parts or something, but recently I heard it was to assess the shop's damage, and then again to get something done with his car. Magnolia seems to know everything about everyone, so she'd shared that bit with me, knowing damn well I've always carried a torch for Sterling.

I wasn't going to get jealous hearing about him going to her shop, but then it's happened multiple times and it has my defenses flying up. Could my brother and the others be trying to get her to do Porn Kings with them for some extra money? Or the more serious question, has she done porn with Sterling? I don't care if she has with the others, but Sterling is a different story. She's gorgeous. I'm not blind, and you'd have to be to not notice her. I have no right to go there with her, or him, really, but I still do regardless.

If only things were easy and I could attach a big glowing sign to him that told the female population to stay the hell away from him. That will never happen, and with the way things have been going where him and I are concerned, there may never be a chance for us to have a shot together. If we did though, would he want it? Would he take it? I know my answer. It's never wavered, and sometimes that bit makes me feel a tad pathetic. I'm that woman you read about lusting after a guy, offering him every bit of my thoughts, and then turning around to lap at the crumbs he leaves behind. It makes him sound a bit like a dick as well, but he's not. If he were, I wouldn't want him so badly, that's for sure.

I adjust my bikini top, spreading the thin sunshine-colored triangles out a bit more. I don't have any upper tan lines, and this color pops against my deep southern tan. I shimmy into a pair of faded cut-off jean shorts, thinking I may be drinking one too many smoothies at work because they're a little tighter than usual. They're shorter than what I'd normally wear as well, but I'm going to be washing cars, so the less material, the better, as far as I'm concerned. I curled my long hair and put it up into a high, messy ponytail, feathering shorter hair to frame my face a bit and kept my makeup light. I'm sure I'll be a hot mess by the time the fundraiser is over, but at least I look semi-cute going into it. I spray the SPF fifty sport sunscreen on my face, then smooth over the rest of me with some lower SPF lotion and decide it's as good as I'm going to get for this thing.

I glance in the mirror, taking myself in briefly. I wanted to go with my red bikini, but I know Dad will say something if I do. I can get away with the yellow one, but if I put on red or white, then Dad will be barking at me to cover up. Not sure what the color matters, but I'm not trying to be embarrassed by it today.

I search out my keys and purse, grabbing a bottle of water as I go. Uncle Jinx is supposed to bring his giant smoker to make some barbecue, and Mom's providing the sweets with Mrs. Savannah to sell as well. Michaela is donating fountain drinks from the pub, and also a portion of certain sales. I'm in for a day full of good food and even better people—those are always my favorites.

I'm not so secretly hoping Sterling will be there. I have my fingers, toes, and everything else crossed that he shows up and notices me before I become too sweaty and grimy. Of course, he should be around since he's a prospect and gets stuck with a bunch of the grunt work. Maybe Heaven above will smile down on me today and have him washing cars beside me, shirtless. It's not like I can ask anyone about his whereabouts without a viable reason or else it'll come off suspicious. I definitely don't want to scare him off before I ever get the chance to get him where I want him. Not to mention people will wonder why I'm looking for him without searching my brother out as well.

I slip on an old pair of black flip-flops and spritz myself with Burberry 'Her' perfume, then grab a towel on my way out the door. I wonder if Sterling will bring his car out to be washed or if he'll have his bike. Probably the motorcycle since the brothers will be there along with their families. I wouldn't mind catching his expression if he did drive his Charger and I got to wash it for him. Though part of me wonders if he'd just tease me about it. I can't seem to get him to separate me from being Ruin's younger sister, but I'm more than that. I'm a woman.

The drive's short to Mooney's Pub, cutting off my rambling thoughts. I turn down my radio as I pull into the parking lot to park off to the side. The bikes are lined up front while Michaela and Sly are usually parked in the back to make more room. We're supposed to be having the car wash over on the opposite side. The club will fill up this side with their families, no doubt. Grabbing my things, I make my way towards the front of the building, past the bikes, smiling and greeting people as I pass them. Living in a town that's in the middle of nowhere has this effect; you sort of know everyone even when you don't want to.

I wave to Michaela and one of her bartenders who's helping her carry some filled Styrofoam cups out along with pitchers. She's set out some plastic chairs, tables, and umbrellas, with the section roped off for the outside drinkers. Charity or not, the pub will probably make a ton of money today. I have a feeling most of the members will be hanging out and drinking here today with everything going on. I wouldn't mind having a beer, but I won't put Michaela on the spot and ask since I'm underage. I know if we were in her backyard, she wouldn't care, but here it could mess with her business, and it's the last thing I want for any person affiliated with the club.

"Hey, Mom. Hey, Savannah. Can I help you two unload?" Mom presses a kiss to my cheek and Savannah leans over to give me a hug.

"You get more beautiful by the day," she says, and Mom agrees.

"Here, love, straighten these out for us." Mom gestures to items they're busily unloading on a fold-out table. They have a shade set up for them, and they'll need it if it gets any warmer today. I fix everything, making it look neater, and manage to swipe a monster cookie bar before taking off to my own job for the day.

We get everything set up, me and Stryker up first to wash cars with Sawyer handling the donations. Sly will be around her, no doubt to make sure no one hassles her over the donations. He's protective of us all. Some of the club girls are supposed to take over in an hour or so to give us a break. The meat smoker's been going with the promise of Jinx's delicious barbecue, and my stomach's already grumbling for a taste.

The first car pulls in. It's covered in dust and mud, definitely needing a wash. I'm ready and waiting with my foamy sponge and bucket. We've run a few hoses over from the two closest businesses, so hopefully we get a system down and get these vehicles in and out. In the meantime, the drivers can check out Jupiter's suped-up Mustang and get her business info, have a free drink, purchase a beer, a plate of food, or something to take with them from Mom's table. It's a pretty sweet setup, if I do say so myself, and even if it seems a bit silly, I'm excited for the day. I'm proud of how everything turned out. I know my father will be happy and proud of me for organizing everything too.

I grin as the driver climbs out. It's a guy I went to school with. He was always nice to me, so I offer a friendly welcome, grateful he's here to show the fundraiser much-needed support. "Hey, Trevor, thanks for stopping by. How've you been?"

We graduated last year, and while I see him occasionally, it's usually while we're with siblings or parents. I wasn't really into the whole 'party scene' where he hung out a lot, I left that up to my brother and saved Mom the extra dose of worry I knew would accompany the late nights. Not that I couldn't go out at all or anything. My parents trusted me and Ruin. I just preferred to work and hang out at the movies or whatever.

His gaze casually rakes over the front of me, a pleased smirk overtaking his mouth. He pulls me in for a close hug, wrapping me into his body tightly before saying, "I'm doing much better now. Damn, you just keep getting better with time. How are you hotter every time I lay eyes on you?" He winks and I can feel my face flush with the compliment. I'm not a prude or anything, it's just that we're around my family. If Dad or Ruin catch Trevor saying stuff like that, he's liable to end up with some flat tires to go along with his clean vehicle. I'm fairly sure customers won't be donating if their vehicles end up getting vandalized before they leave the parking lot.

I laugh it off, as I head for his car. "Glad to hear it. Thanks for coming out to support the fundraiser. It's appreciated. Sawyer's at that table taking donations. There's also free coke's if you're thirsty." I'm not sure what else I should say in return. I'm flattered, but he's not really my type. I always remember him having a girlfriend before, so maybe that was why he never came on so strong back then? Who knows, and besides, if I'm being honest about it, I don't care. There's one guy that's had my attention, and I doubt that detail will change anytime soon, if ever.

I've just watched Stryker spray the car with the hose and put my soapy sponge on the roof when the rumble of motorcycles vibrate around us. The sound is like a beacon, calling to my soul. The wind, road, and exhaust is in my blood. There's something about it that comforts me. It always has.

ZZ Top blares out of the large speaker in the back of Jinx's truck, and the smell of barbecue permeates the air. Mix it with the throaty pipes from the club's motorcycles and it has me comfortable, singing along and swaying my hips with the music as I wash. I'm in my own little world, trying to do a decent job, when a bike's engine revs loudly before going silent. I turn around in time to catch Trevor staring where my ass was moments prior. He sends me another grin and a thumbs-up when he meets my eyes, but I don't hold his for long.

My attention pins on the pissed-off biker storming across the cement, clad in his jeans and vest proclaiming him a prospect of the Kings of Carnage MC. Dropping the sponge, I unknowingly push my chest out and cock my hip. My soaked hand rests on my waist, while my brows raise. It takes Sterling all of a few seconds to cross from his bike to Trevor. He gets in the guy's face and snarls something before stalking towards me, anger clouding his gaze. He snatches my hand, his firm grip tugging me behind him.

I follow right along because I have no idea what the hell is happening right now. Is something wrong? "Sterling?" I attempt to get out, but his pace is far too quick with his long legs, and it has me shutting my mouth, jogging to keep up. Something must've gotten into him because he's never acted this way in the past. My curiosity is killing me to know what's going on in his mind.

He stops at his bike, spinning around, glaring but remains silent. He yanks his obsidian half-shell helmet from the seat and not so softly plops it on my head. He connects the snap and then is climbing on his bike. He tugs me towards the back and I swing my leg over, perching on the tiny bit of seat he's left for me. I wrap my arms around his waist, not sure what's gotten into him all of a sudden. He caresses my thigh, then lifts his middle finger to Trevor, barks something towards Saint that I don't catch, and then revs his engine.

I tighten my hold in time for him to release the brake and take off. I've never ridden on Sterling's motorcycle like this. There were times when we were younger, if I begged enough, he'd give me short rides on his dirt bike around my parents' property, but never like this. As far as I know, no one has ever ridden bitch on the back of his bike, and it has my stomach twirling with excitement and confusion.

I hold on, not shying away from wrapping my hands around his waist. I've wanted to ride his bike since he bought it, I've fantasized many times of this day. Sure, it hadn't gone down the same way, but that detail means nothing. What matters is it's happening, and I finally have him in my arms, where I've always wanted him.

Sterling doesn't have a shirt on under his cut; he never wears one. The struggle is real not to run my hands over his abdomen and chest, feeling him up like some creeper. It's what I want though. Jesus, I crave it fiercely. He's warm, his skin sun-kissed and hot from riding around in the Georgia heat. He's got a sexy tan, one that makes it seem like his cut is a permanent part of him. Then there's his scent drawing me in, like my personal aphrodisiac to him. I lean in, inhaling deeply, not ever getting enough. He's all road, wind, and spicy cologne teasing my nostrils, making my pussy clench wantonly.

I wish he'd pull over and kiss me. I'd be down for removing my clothes as well if he'd allow it. He could fuck me over his bike on the side of the road. Or better yet, he could sit steady and let me crawl on him to ride his cock until he's groaning his release for all of Georgia to hear. Unfortunately, I don't think that's one fantasy I can anticipate coming true anytime soon, no matter how badly I silently will it to.

He's said absolutely nothing since we left the pub parking lot, and it's driving me nuts to not say anything about it. I don't like the quiet, especially when I feel like there's so much that needs to be said aloud between us. Does this mean what I think it does? Do I dare hope? Will he finally see me as a woman, one he desires, or will it be the same as before? Surely, he wouldn't go caveman on me in front of everyone and drag me away without it meaning something significant. Nearly the entire club was there, I'm sure they saw everything plain as day. How will he explain what happened, and if it's not about me and him, then what the hell did I miss?

"Sterling," I say, wanting to ask him. He takes the curve a little quickly, steering us in the direction of the Kings of Carnage's clubhouse. I'm enjoying this ride, and if we're not going to do what I'd like us to, then I want to know what's going through his mind. It'd be nice to have some sort of heads-up, before dealing with the repercussions of his actions. He doesn't say anything in response, irritating me. Rather than allow him to ignore me, I shout his name, demanding some sort of acknowledgment as my hands hold him a bit tighter, making him feel my touch.

Sometimes standing up for yourself can be as simple as waking away from a situation that does not support or honor your self-worth.
-@THESMOKINGPROPHET

Sterling

I'm so fucking pissed inside, I'm boiling. The stupid douche back at the pub had some big fucking nerve to be staring at Leigh like he was in front of her family and the club. Just who the hell does he think he is to disrespect her like that? Did he think the members and anyone else would find it cute to witness him watching Leigh like she was a goddamn ice cream cone, licking his lips and adjusting himself like a disgusting dog? Frankly, I'm fucking stunned no one opened their mouths about it before I'd had a chance to watch for a few beats. It took me no time to see what was going on, where it was heading, and everything in me to stop from caving his damn face in.

No one will ever disrespect Leigh like that in my presence, and they'd damn sure better not try it in my absence. I will hunt a motherfucker down and make him hurt for it. I've done it in the past for her and I'd do it again. She'll never know as much. That's between me and her mom.

I have to take her to the clubhouse. There's no way I can go to her apartment or my trailer. I'd end up fucking her just to prove a point...It's wrong. She's not mine to beat my chest over, and I shouldn't think of her in that sort of way. It's getting worse though, the temptation is there and it's harder and harder to turn away from going for what I want. I'll be damned if some flippin' yo-yo like Trevor Billings gets his grubby paws on Leigh, it'll be over my dead fucking body, that much I know for sure.

"Sterling?" she calls over my shoulder. Her sweet melody only angers me further for losing control around her. She shouldn't have witnessed me behave like that, I could've upset her, and that's the last thing I'd ever want. I'm trying to protect her, to look out for her and her wellbeing. Surely, she can appreciate as much. At least, I hope she can. I'd want someone else to do it for Sawyer, only not have the sort of thoughts about her as I do with Leigh.

"Damn it, stop talking, Boo!" I holler over the wind and my pipes. I need to concentrate, and having her firm little body pressed snuggly against my back has me doing everything but that. I want to pull over, bend her over my bike, and fuck her until she screams she'll take no other cock but mine. Christ. I'm a mess, and this desire I have for her will only make Chaos bury me. It's never been an issue before, never even mentioned to me because of Stryker. He's closer to Leigh's age, so Chaos and Dad were always concerned he'd end up interested in Leigh at some point. They never thought twice about me being the one who'd end up craving her. I don't think anyone around the club would expect it.

"Fuck!" I roar, allowing the road and wind to claim some of my torment. I hate losing my shit in front of her, but I feel like I'm ready to explode. I'm lost, my thoughts zig-zagging all over the place, and she's firmly in the middle of them all.

"Sterling, please!" she calls, and her voice crushes me inside. I've upset her, and it cuts me. I pull into the club, kick stand toed down in a rush, ignition off, and I hold my hand out to help her from my motorcycle. Once she's safely off beside me, I haul ass striding for the club. She jogs after me, but I'm quicker and make it into the quiet bar to find Chaos before she can get in front of me.

"Do you see her? What she's wearing?" I say, years of respect instilled in me. Even so, it has me struggling not to scream the words with hostility. This is his daughter; he shouldn't let her out of the fucking house dressed like this without a man on her for protection. Someone would tempt their fate, I know it. Look at what just went down with Bruce, and now she's nearly naked with no personal protection. Leigh is far too beautiful already, but toss in her tits and curvy little ass without a guard dog at her heels and it's a recipe for disaster. I'm around her damn near every day and I still struggle with keeping my hands to myself.

His lips settle into a frown, his jaw flexing as he clenches his teeth together. He stands, swiftly strolling towards me until we're toe-to-toe. I'm no kid anymore. I'm the same height as him, maybe an inch or so taller, but that means absolutely nothing when it comes to Chaos. He's the prez, and he's lived the life. He has the experience and knowledge that I'm nowhere close to possessing, and to be honest, it's intimidating as fuck.

"Hm," he grumbles, and my throat feels tight. He's fucking

pissed. "I see my little girl wearing her bathing suit because she was washing cars for a fundraiser that she organized herself. She was helping, like she said she would. You telling me you see something different, *prospect*?"

Fuck. This is one helluva test. Releasing a tense breath, I say, "She was dancing around and singing. Shaking her hips. She barely has any material covering her body." My jaw clenches before admitting, "Everyone would've been blind not to see it. I'm just brave enough to say it aloud."

"As they should be. Brave, hmm." He grunts, flicking his gaze over me briefly. His brow scrunches as he pins his dominating stare on his daughter, but she doesn't wilt under his pressure. "Leigh? Got anything to say for yourself?"

She shrugs. "I was singing ZZ Top and scrubbing a car, sue me." Her hands fly up in exasperation. "I wasn't paying attention to anything else, just trying to help."

"That so?" he says, his icy glower resting back on me. "You got something else to say, *son*?" The label has so much weight to it, coming from a man I've looked at like a second father for as long as I can remember. At least he's not calling me prospect anymore.

"Trevor Billings was enjoying the show a little too much. She should have a shirt on at the very least." I fling my hand in her chest direction. "Cover those up."

His nostrils flair as he leans in, nose nearly touching my own. It's taking everything in me not to shit a brick right now. I don't want him pissed, but he needs to know I won't back down when I'm right about something either. I want my patch, and being the prez, he'll respect me more if I have a pair between my legs and don't act like a scared little bitch. "Sounds like you were enjoying it too. We got an issue here, *boy*?"

Shit, that's worse than him calling me prospect. I swallow, deciding I want to keep the nuts between my legs.

Seeing as it's his daughter, I back down, flashing my perturbed stare to Leigh. Of course, she's standing there in her now-dry bikini top and tiny shorts, stomach and half her tits on display. It's enough to drive any man wild with lust and frustration.

I pull a Bash. I release a loud, "Fuck!" and stride away, punching the wall a few times on my way out. Stryker is like our father when it comes to losing his temper—not me, usually, but where Leigh's concerned...it seems Bash lives inside me after all. It eats away at me that she's seen me fly off the handle yet again today. This is a record for me, one I won't be forgetting anytime soon. Add into it that Chaos has seen me lose my shit as well, and I know it wont be the end of this conversation between us.

Climbing onto my bike, I forgo the helmet still resting on Leigh's perfect head. The engine rumbles as the club door swings open again. Leigh's there, tears trailing down her cheeks, and it's my breaking point. Releasing the clutch, I have to get the fuck out of here. I need far, far away from Leigh, or else I'll meet my maker, and I'm not ready to give her up completely. I may willingly give up shit for the club, but in the end, I'm still a bit selfish when it comes to her, no matter how hard I fight it. When did it even become this serious of a thing for me?

Ruin pulls in, signaling me to wait before I have a chance to leave the parking lot. "What the hell happened, Spade?" he calls over the rumble of our idling bikes. He's probably still hungover from partying it up, celebrating. He finally got his patch sewn on, and I couldn't be happier for him. Perhaps I wouldn't be feeling so alone in this moment if he hadn't, but it is what it is.

"I know you saw what she had on," I return, not having made it fully out of the parking lot.

His forehead screws up in confusion. "Who? What are you talking about?"

"Your sister. She was half naked, acting like she had no worries, while being drooled over."

He shrugs. "I didn't realize she was there yet. I pulled in on the opposite side of you guys, since Tyra's car was over there. You saw me veer off after you told me you'd be back. At least, I thought you did."

I nod, frustrated. "Fuck. Yeah, it was Saint beside me," I mutter. "You can't sit here and make me believe that I'm the only person in the club who saw her shaking her ass wearing next to nothing though. Every motherfucker in this club notices her! You need to open your eyes, bro. Leigh isn't a little girl anymore. She's got the body to prove it, and everyone sees it but you and Chaos. She's a woman, and every single man in this club wants her. I'm not losing my head, man, I'm not." I can't be.

"What'd she have on? I thought she was showing up to wash cars. That's what Mom said."

I nod towards the club. She's sitting on the bench out front, arms crossed, wearing a sexy pout. Fucking brat. "Shorts so short, her ass cheeks were hanging out the bottom, and that fucking tiny bikini."

He stares at her a beat then says, "She loves that yellow swimsuit. She's had it for a while now." He acts like it's no big deal, when in fact, it's a huge fucking deal—to me. "You're telling me *you* noticed her though, aren't you?" His brow shoots up, same as Chaos' had.

I give the look right back at him. "Everyone, Ruin, everyone. She should be in real fucking clothes around so many men. I caught dipshit watching her, adjusting his dick while she shook her ass, and I knew he was planning to fuck her. I couldn't allow that to happen. I wouldn't."

He stares at me quizzically, quietly. Eventually, he asks, "Does Chaos know she rode on the back of your bike? That you brought her here because of her outfit?"

I offer a jerky nod and rub my hand over my face. "I made her go into the clubhouse to show him. He had to see her for himself why I was pissed."

He chuckles, shaking his head. "Oh fuck. I'm guessing Chaos agreed with you, and it's why he left you breathing after that shit?"

"Not entirely," I reluctantly admit, and Ruin's eyes widen.

Leigh stomps in our direction, securing the helmet back onto her sexy head as she struts her curvy ass to my bike. "Get me out of here," she demands, looking alluring as fuck with her cheeks and chest flushed scarlet. "I can't believe you did this. You owe me after this stunt," she nearly hisses with her anger.

Fuck me sideways, she's beyond sexy when she's pissed off. Ruin interrupts, "Are you mental, Leigh? You're not riding around town on the back of Sterling's fucking bike. He won't allow it, and neither will Chaos. Go back inside before Chaos becomes really pissed."

Speaking of, the club door opens, with Chaos coming out. He lights up a cigarette, watching us in the parking lot. He's probably plotting my death as we speak. Leigh glowers at her older brother and proclaims, "I can make my own decisions, thank you very much. Worry about why Tyra isn't riding with you right now, not about what I'm doing."

She pins her stare on me next. "Either you take me, or I'll call the guy who just gave me his number," she taunts, and jealousy curls deep in my gut. I've never been this person, one who loses control over a woman or has an ounce of possessiveness feeding my soul.

"Leigh, stop fucking around already," "Ru huffs, and I say nothing.

She takes my silence as a sign of agreement and swings her leg over the back, hands clutching me while she climbs on. I meet Ruin's gaze, his more tormented as the repercussions finally begin to sink in and I don't shove her away. "Don't do this, Sterling. You're going to fuck everything up, and you're so close. Make her get off and go talk to my father," he warns.

I squeeze my temples and admit, "It's too late. There's no going back." I give my bike some gas as Leigh wraps her arms tighter around my middle.

Ruin and Chaos watch us go, my heart thundering away in my chest. It's not beating hard because of the potential danger I'm facing. No, it's all thanks to having the club princess's touch on me once more. I was already beginning to miss it, and that's got me even more confused. Her dainty hands slide under my cut, rubbing my bare abdomen, while her tight body is snuggled up against my frame. Full tits press into the leather on my back, and fuck, I wish I had nothing at all between us.

There's no stopping the beast I just unleashed by putting this bitch on the back of my bike. I may as well touch, fuck, and feel my fill, as I know Chaos will come for me. It may not be tonight, but I know my time will surely run out. He's the prez, after all, and I just took his daughter.

I ride without knowing where to go or what to do. We stay like that, her glued to me while I follow the road for an hour or so, feeling perplexed and lost. I have all these feelings trapped inside me that I don't know what to do with. It's like they've come out of nowhere and hit me from left field. I have no right to act like I did today and that has my mind fucked up. Leigh isn't mine. She can't be... ever. I'm protective over her, I always have been, but this? It's next level, and if I don't watch it, I'm going to ruin everything. Not only with our friendship, but with my club patch and the relationship between our two families.

I have to do the right thing, no matter how much I want to fight it. I need to reel it the fuck in and be a man, do what's required of me. I won't be selfish and take what I want. It's not who I am. I can't be. Eventually, I pull into her apartment parking lot, having spent enough time on my decision to make peace with it. I come to a stop, toeing my kickstand down. I climb off, holding my hand out to help her off as well. She can do it herself, but she shouldn't have to.

She offers me a shaky smile, her gaze confused. I did that, put that uncertainty in her eyes, and I fucking hate it. She allows me to lead her to her door, but I pause there on her stoop. I step closer, pushing her against the wall next to her door. I raise my hand, placing it above her head, and lean in. Meeting her stare, I say seriously, "I'm sorry for earlier. I lost it and with you. I seem to have a shorter fuse. You're special and should be treated as such."

Her eyes widen, not expecting to hear that leave my lips. "Sterling—" she begins, but I cut her off.

"It's the truth," I murmur, dipping my head. I slant my mouth over hers, our lips fusing together in a touch that should've happened long ago but was never given the option. Her mouth welcomes mine, her tongue tangling with mine, and it's more than it should be. Her taste...it's like coming home. Warm, sweet, and needy. She's everything I desire, yet can't possess. She's forbidden and that title doesn't sit well with my rule-breaking soul.

My thumb softly caresses her chin, having to touch her smooth, tan flesh in a small way. I pull back, breaking the tender moment and profess, "This will never happen again, Boo. You're not mine and you'll never be. I have no claim to you." With those heart-crushing words, I spin on my heel for my bike.

The engine roars, loudly blanketing the night in my brooding anger. I'm not one to give up easily, and I have a feeling this decision will be one to haunt me long into the future.

THE ENTIRE RIDE TO DROP THESE GUNS OFF, I CAN'T GET LEIGH OUT OF MY head. It's been like that since she showed up at my place crying. It fucks with me inside, along with the knowledge I'll be expected to speak to Chaos about it again when I return.

I cast a side glance towards Dad, taking in his strong, confident appearance. There're enough weapons in the truck in front of us to put us all away for a while, but you'd never know as much by Dad's expression. I suppose that's how he's managed to do this for so long, along with not selling to shoddy motherfuckers. Someday, I hope I can look at the world with as much confidence and assurance as he does. Until then, I'll keep crashing through life, attempting not to get killed by my best friend's father. Fun times.

Twenty minutes later and we're pulling into Hooligan territory. We've sold to them before so I'm not sweating it too much. It'd be different rolling up on an MC I've never met before. Dad nods to me as we're coming up on the entrance to their clubhouse. He always has me fall back a bit. He says it's in case there's any sort of ambush set up, I have a better chance of getting away. I don't agree with him, but if it makes the old man feel better, then so be it.

Everything's the same as before, so I pull in, stopping on the opposite side of the truck in front of the massive 'Cajun Hooligans

MC' spray-paint job a member did. I'm not knocking it. The guy's an artist and his graffiti looks sick as fuck along the building. Mako climbs out from behind the wheel as North comes outside to greet us. He and Saint rode about ten minutes ahead of us as lookouts. It's just another reason why the Kings are who they are. They're smart and careful, so they don't get caught or shot by rivals or cops.

"Brother," Dad greets, and North returns it. He swiftly glances over me and Mako before telling Mako to get his prospect ass in the truck and pull around the back. We've been going damn near eight hours, so I know Mako's sore being stuffed in the truck. I am as well from the long, straight ride. It felt good cruising down the road, hair in the wind, but I'm also stiff and need to walk around. Any longer and we'd be sporting chapped asses, not that I'll admit as much to Dad. I'd never hear the end of it, and he'd tell the brothers.

"All of us?" I ask.

North grunts, "Yeah. Hurry the fuck up. Got some cold beer back there waiting for your delicate pretty-boy ass."

Dad chuckles at him ribbing me. I snort, leaving my bike parked to walk alongside the truck. Dad does the same so he must need to stretch out as well. "Damn," I sigh in relief. "North wasn't fucking around," I comment, taking in the setup. There's a metal trough filled to the brim with beer and ice. There're propane burners going with massive pots full of something boiling, and half-naked women setting up an oversized table and tiki torches.

"These Cajuns know how to welcome some folks, that's for damn sure," Dad mutters as the club's president comes out to greet us wearing a grin.

"Kings!" he boasts with a deeper drawl than our own. "Welcome. Everything make it here all right?"

He shakes Dad's hand, shifting his attention on him and North, ignoring me and Mako as Saint comes to stand with us. They act like we don't exist, being the lowest on the totem pole, but I don't mind. I'm used to it, having been prospecting for a while. I know we'll get stuck cleaning the shit up tonight with the Hooligan prospects, but I'll get a belly full of food and beer, so I'm not complaining. It's one step closer to my patch, and right now, I need all the good graces I can get with Chaos.

Saint grins. "Tonight's going to be wild. They've got some bomb-ass pussy inside." He rubs his hands together. "Hoping I get a taste of a few."

Mako shakes his head. "You know we don't get club ass, not even from our own club."

Saint shrugs. "Who knows, maybe these Cajuns are friendlier when it comes to everything." I wouldn't hold my breath, but don't say as much.

The night kicks off as I expected it would, and ends much the same way. The prospects get stuck cleaning up everything, and all the pussy is snatched up by the brothers. I was too tired to crave a bitch on my cock anyhow. The porn has jaded me a bit as well. Sex isn't the first thing on my mind like it would be if I were a normal dude my age around club sluts. Don't get me wrong, if I were motivated by a particular woman, then things would be different, I'm sure of it.

THE NEXT DAY, NORTH, SAINT, MAKO, DAD, AND I ALL HEAD BACK FOR Georgia. The weather's still mild, but this is the south; it's humid no matter if it's spring, summer, or fall. I can tell Dad has something to say to me, and he doesn't hold back for long. We pull in to top off our tanks and grab some grub.

We stand around the back of the truck, stretching our legs. Dad and I are out here first with our subs. The others are grabbing drinks and whatever else they wanted. "I've heard a few things," he begins.

I grunt, having just taken a large bite of my sandwich. Not that I want to discuss this, regardless of my mouth being full or not.

He drinks his fountain Sprite and continues. "Some shit go down at the carwash that I managed to miss? Chaos told me part of it, but it didn't sound like you. What's going on?"

I shrug, chewing up my food. I watch as he takes a bite and finally admit, "I may've overreacted slightly. I think it was before you showed up." His brow raises. "Leigh was there with barely any clothes on." His other brow hikes as well, and I can't help but huff. "It's not like that. She was in a goddamn bikini, shaking her ass, while some guy rubbed his dick, making comments and shit."

"What the hell? I haven't heard anything about a guy having his cock out. Your mother should've told me."

I shake my head. "Not like that. He had his shit in his pants." I take another bite as the guys come back outside, striding towards us.

Dad chuckles, shaking his head. "You got that angry over someone adjusting his dick? This is Leigh we're talking about. She's a sweetheart, I doubt she was giving him a striptease or some shit. The fuck happened, Sterling? Chaos said you lost it, acted out and what not."

North casts his gaze between us and I say, "You were there at that time. You see that fuck nut rubbing himself while Leigh was dancing and washing his car?"

He releases a breath, setting his stuff down on the tailgate as Mako and Saint perch on the sidewalk curb and dig into their food.

"Look, I'm not getting in the middle of this shitshow, kid. I will say, though, that if I saw that go down with my daughter, I'd have been heated."

My hands fly out to the sides. "Thank you! Fucking Christ," I say. "Everyone's kept their mouths shut like I was imagining stuff, but I knew I wasn't the only one wanting to teach that punk bitch a lesson."

Dad's eyes clench closed for a beat. "Fuck. This isn't good. I need to figure out how to smooth this over." His stare pins me. "You need to speak to Chaos when we get home. Hammer this shit out and move on. Explain to him you were protecting her and he'll understand. I'd want Ruin to do the same for Sawyer."

It takes everything in me not to snort. If only my old man knew the thoughts I was having about Leigh. He'd damn sure not want my best friend feeling the same way about my little sister. The last thing I was thinking of when I snatched Leigh out of there was about protection. More like I wanted to commit murder and fuck her all in the same beat. Blind, jealous rage had consumed me, and it was jaw-dropping to say the least.

People aren't always going to be there for you. That's why you learn to handle things on your own.

-lifequotesru.net

Sterling

I hate the way I miss her. I shouldn't think of her as much as I do. It's wrong, yet I can't seem to stop. It's getting worse with each day. I remember the way her body fit snugly behind mine, how right it felt to have her on the back of my bike. I want to ride by her place, knowing she's not at work yet, but I can't. I have to go straight to the clubhouse to check in.

I turn off at the MC, following Dad and North, with Saint and Mako right behind me. Mako parks the truck off to the side, while Saint and I park next to the other prospect bikes. Dad and North pull right up front next to Ruin and Chaos' bikes. I won't try to lie to myself. Seeing Chaos' bike damn near has me shitting my pants.

At least Dad is here this time. I know things won't get too crazy with him around. He and Chaos feed off each other's energy, and if one is calm, the other usually remains that way as well.

"Brothers," is boomed as we enter. "Prospects," prez acknowledges all of us. "Any issues, Bash?" he asks.

Dad shakes his head. "Nah, the run was easy. Good ride and no problems. They're a wild bunch for sure."

Chaos grins, smacking Dad on his back. "That's what I like to hear. Let's get a beer and you can catch me up." They head for the bar and I stay back, seeking Ruin. Him, Bear, and Crow aren't around so they must be handling something out back or in the garage. I leave to take a piss, and when I return, Dad waives me over. They've moved to some couches by the pool table they're always playing on.

Chaos gestures. "Have a seat, Sterling. We need to talk."

I swallow and offer a jerky nod. I've known Chaos my entire life, and it's not that I necessarily fear him...I respect him. That's what makes this situation difficult. "All right." I plop my tired, road-weary ass down, and give him my full attention.

"You left with Leigh on the back of your bike," he begins. Dad's brows jump.

So I didn't mention that to him earlier. I sorta left out some shit 'cause I didn't want to discuss it then. Fuck. I don't want to deal with this right now either, but I don't have much of a choice any longer it seems.

"Considering that spot is normally empty, that's a fairly big statement coming from you. Granted, the brothers weren't around, but it still must mean something."

I hope she didn't tell him anything. I doubt she would though. Leigh is trustworthy when it comes to me. She's always been that way. “It’s not like that,” I start off, and he shoots me a look that says he thinks I’m full of shit. He’s right because it is like that. I want her.

“It better not be any sort of way except brotherly, you feel me? My daughter’s nineteen years old and doesn’t need a motherfuckin’ King beating on his chest over her aside from me. You hear me?”

I exhale, keeping my mouth locked tight. This isn’t a conversation after all; it’s merely a warning. He wants me to stay away from her, and won’t hear anything else on the matter. Well, his message is received loud and clear, and I’ll do what’s necessary to keep the peace, whether I like it or not. And, for the record, I don’t like it.

“Yes, sir,” I eventually get out, knowing my father expects that response from me, as does Chaos. This is going to suck ass.

You are far too smart to be the only
thing standing in your way.
-Jennifer J. Freeman

Leigh

I've seen the videos of Sterling. I've watched them all. I don't know why I didn't think of this sooner. I bribed Crow. He'd been acting a little weird around the club lately, and I happened to point it out. He was scattered at my acknowledgment and said he'd do anything to prove he was just like all the other prospects. Poor guy is newer around the club, so I took advantage of it. He offers me a thumbs-up, as he stands behind the monitor with the audio and camera controls. If he had any idea of what Ruin or my father would do to him if they saw him here helping me, he'd be running for the hills.

He sent the text to Sterling for me, letting him know there's a new girl signed up and he's being called in to fuck me for the next Porn Kings flick. I wanted Tyra to paint my face like she does with the guys, make me sexy and savage, but no one can know about this—not even her. My brother would kill me, as would my father. They'd be so pissed, I'd never hear the end of it. So here I am, in a black fitted mask. It's not perfect but will do the trick. The only thing on the material is two glowing Xs where my eyes should be and a fucked-up sinister smile. It glows neon green and is a bit blinding from the inside. The fabric over my eyes and mouth is a thin black mesh with tiny holes, the same color as the rest. I'll be able to see him, but not the other way around. Sterling will never know who I am unless I speak.

I remove my clothes, exposing my naked body to the room and the cameras. I dust a bit of edible powdered body glitter over my nipples that I brought along. It tastes like vanilla frosting, which I know Sterling loves. My bikini lines tattle, telling on me that I tan topless on the balcony at my apartment. Not that anyone will guess it's me. Only my closest friend knows I have a penchant for tanning in the nude because she does it as well. Magnolia's always been a bit of a bad influence, but that's one of the many reasons why I love being her friend.

I lie back on the bed and wait, but not for long. My nerves twist my stomach with anticipation and excitement. I've waited far too long to have this man, to feel him skin to skin. Finally, one of my fantasies is going to come true. The best thing out of this is, if we don't work well together, he'll never know it was me and we can keep being friends. Not that I doubt our sexual chemistry. If anything, I imagine it'll be positively sinful. The pull between us is natural and it's been there for a long time.

The door opens and Sterling swaggers inside. He's got a proud strut, like he owns everything and gives zero fucks. It's alluring, and I find it hard to look away, whether my vision is fuzzy from the mask or not. His gaze finds me, mouth dropping open in surprise. He's not used to anyone having the upper hand, not even in here from what I've heard. People don't talk much at the clubhouse, but they do slip up at times, and I've managed to catch some details about Sterling's sure attitude in his 'work' so to speak.

I smirk behind the mask and move to stand, giving him a better view of my curvy body. After his tantrum over my clothes at the car wash, I know he's had to notice me and has been paying attention to my luscious curves. It's his lucky day as he'll get up close and personal with them all. I step to him, reaching to peel his shirt away before he can protest. He goes with it, his brows practically in his hairline. I continue to undress him, relishing in the task as i move lower and peer up at him from my knees. He can't see my expression though, nor the adoration reflecting in my gaze...only the creepy mask. My sense of protection, allowing me to finally be as brazen as I wish with him.

His long, thick cock juts out proudly before me. He's big and hard, making my mouth water to taste him. I didn't think that through with this disguise, however. Hopefully, there'll be a repeat where I can take him in my mouth and taste him properly. The thought alone of me worshipping him with my tongue has me growing slicker between my thighs.

He grabs for a shiny wrapped condom from a full bowl placed off to the side, along with his cryptic skull mask. He pulls it over his head quickly, and I impatiently tug him along behind me. I lift my hand in the air, spinning my finger to signal the music to be turned on. Crow obliges, "Dizzy" by Missio floods the room. As soon as I'd heard this song for the first, I knew I wanted to fuck Sterling to it.

I pause at the foot of the bed, shoving him so he falls backward onto the dark bedspread. "Fuck," he curses. I've seen how he is. He's a Porn King. *A King*. He's in charge. Well, fuck that. Today, he's mine. Wasting no time, I straddle his legs, slowly working my way up his body while watching him roll the condom over his impressive length.

"You want me?" he rasps, the heat coating his timbre. He's in a trance as he stares me down. Inch by inch, I crawl until the tip of his cock rubs from the top of my head, over the front of my cloth-covered face, pausing for me to nudge it with my mouth. Jesus, I wish my lips weren't covered right now. he's the most sinful fucking man I've ever had my hands on before.

He groans and I grin. I rub my mouth over the head of his cock, teasing, then continue my perusal. My chin moves, running up his full length, and his fists clench, not used to practicing patience in his pornos. He wants this badly enough he's waiting me out. My nails slide up his abdomen, leaving behind pink trail marks. I eagerly take in his flexed muscles, gaining my balance on my knees to hover over his length.

"Now," he orders, and I stop, wagging my finger at him. He's not a spoiled brat in here. It'll be my way, and then he'll get his orgasm. Besides, I'm enjoying myself far too much, finally getting to explore his body after dreaming of it for so long. He'll have to be patient a bit longer. If I weren't so horny for him, I'd be taking even longer to worship his form.

"Naughty," I manage to make my voice a bit velvety, and he draws in a quick breath. Leaning back on my hands, I pop my groin up, spreading my thighs wide so he can see everything. He needs to know exactly what he does to me, how much his sexiness affects my body too.

"Fuck," he grinds the curse out again with a heavy sigh. He must've noticed my pierced pussy. Once I saw his Jacob's ladder in his videos, I knew I needed one too, and got my hood pierced. It was painful, but the best decision. It's brought me countless pleasures. When he had me on the back of his bike, it was a struggle not to come from the vibrations alone. I was pissed when we ended up at the clubhouse and not at one of our places. We should've fucked that day. He and I both know it, yet he pretends like he doesn't feel what I do. He can lie to himself all he wants, but the truth will come out. I'm about to prove my point here and now, just how perfect we fit together.

"You believed you were the only one? Tsk, tsk, bad boy," I taunt in a whisper.

He reaches towards the sliver of pink flesh, lightly trailing the pad of his finger over the silver jewelry, and I moan. He takes the opportunity to rim my opening, but I allow him to get no further. Dropping my pelvis, I lean forward and rub my pussy lips around the head of his cock. I wish I could feel him bareback the entire time, but I know he only fucks with a condom. After watching all of his videos multiple times, you begin to notice all the little things. Like the light tan freckle he has on his left hip bone area. One day, I'll kiss that spot. I've promised myself, and I'm determined to make it come true.

"Who are you?" he utters, caught up in the sensations.

Who am I indeed...Only the woman who's been lusting after him for years. Would he freak out if I told him I'm his? I am, but I don't think he's ready to hear that just yet. I don't want to blindside him with a dose of truth at the moment, but rather, lure him in further so he'll accept our fate when the time is right.

"I'm what you've been missing," I claim confidently instead, and sink over his thick length. I cry out, his piercings along his large cock like nothing I've ever felt before. My eyes begin to roll heavenward, but I fight myself to keep them trained on him instead. I can't miss a mere moment of us being together.

Holy shit. I understand why the fucker's so cocky and sure of himself now. "Oh!" I choke out as his hands claim my hips, shifting us to hit deeper inside. At this rate, I may have his cock sitting in the back of my throat, he feels so damn deep inside me. I sit a moment, just rocking and trying to hold back from coming. I attempt to move a beat later, gritting my teeth as I climb my way back upwards, then rotate my hips.

He groans, motivating me to keep moving the same way, before suddenly dropping down hard. We call out in sync, and I silently rejoice. I keep up the pattern. I don't know how much time passes, lost in our bodies finally joining. The lyrics play on a loop in my mind, reflecting my personal thoughts. I ignore the fact we're being recorded and watched by Crow. In my mind, it's only me and Sterling, and everything's the way it should be.

"Where have you been all my life?" he asks too low for the camera to pick up. In my next breath, he's flipping me onto my back, him hovering above me, nestled between my thighs. and I'm surrounded by his manly scent, driving me wild. He's so much better than I ever could've imagined. "I'm the wolf in here, sweetheart," he warns with a quick thrust forward, making me gasp for my next breath. "Don't get it twisted, sugar." He draws out to his tip, then dives back in. It feels insanely good.

I lean up until my cloth-covered lips touch his masked mouth. I lick his perfect pout through the material and declare, "Perhaps you're not the only predator in the room, *sugar*."

With a growl, his hand comes to the middle of my chest,

shoving me back down. He holds me to the bed as his hips pick up speed, pistoning his cock in and out of me, hard and deep. In mere moments, I'm screaming through my orgasm, and he's roaring with his release. This was no Porn Kings movie. This was him and I—fucking. No one else was in the room with us. As far as I'm concerned, everything else disappeared but *him.*

"Sterling," I murmur his name, lost in a blissful bubble as I begin to come down. Mini zaps of pleasure still hit me randomly, keeping me sated and on edge all at once. I think I came twice in a row, if I'm honest with myself, and I'm too out of it to realize I've slipped up until he's yanking my mask from my face. Stunned would be an understatement, once he discovers my face underneath. He jumps off the bed so fast, you'd think his ass was on fire.

"What the fuck!" he roars. "I can't believe this shit! You want me dead? Is that it? You want Chaos or Ruin to fucking kill me? Goddamn it, Leigh!"

"W-what? What are you talking about?" I ask. My eyes shoot toward Crow. He shakes his head, letting me know he has the cameras off, but smartly he remains silent and away from Sterling's wrath. I know he would never physically hurt me, ever, but Crow may catch some of the blowback on this, and he doesn't deserve it for merely being stuck in the wrong place at the wrong time. Some brilliant plan of mine, it seems.

Sterling points, peering at me as if I've betrayed him. I guess in a sense, I did. I withheld my identity, nothing else, but I had no choice if I wanted to be with him. "You can't be on camera!" he shouts, then his gaze moves from me to pin on Crow. "Fucking delete it. All of it. Right now. This never fucking happened."

Crow begins to nod and I leap towards him. "Don't you dare! We have a deal, Crow. You better keep it," I threaten. Who is this person right now? I'm not a blackmailer...but, when it comes to Sterling, I have no boundaries. I'll do anything to get my time with him, and that includes betrayal and coercion. I'm the KOC president's daughter. I was raised to be strong and smart.

Sterling glances between us a few times, appearing overwhelmed before eventually stopping on me. He shakes his head, gaze wounded but furious. "Of all people," he begins, running his hand through his hair. "I never would've expected this from you."

"Oh no?" I toss my hands out to my sides, over it all, watching him yank his clothes on in a rush. "Of course not...why am I not surprised. And why the hell *not* me?" The last question comes out in a rage-filled scream as he pulls his stupid chunky black biker boots on. My heart and pride are feeling a bit battered after his reaction to what I thought was epic between us. Things are going to be awkward now.

He meets my gaze and divulges, "Because I always believed you were better. I was stupid to think the club hadn't touched you that deeply. My fucking bad."

I'm struck speechless and trying not to cry in front of him while I stand here, soul bared and body naked. I've never been so raw for someone before in my life, and it's turned into a giant shitshow. I have no clue what to say or do to salvage this. If it can even be saved at this point.

"You want the porn? Fine. Fucking keep it, load it, do whatever the fuck you want with it. 'Cause fuck me and what I think, right? Fuck *my* consent," he says, sounding a bit broken, and leaves.

I scramble to put clothes on to catch him, to apologize or do something, but it's useless. The roar of his bike is loud and clear before I'm able to even get my shorts buttoned. It sounds so final, and it has my heart hammering rapidly, feeling like the organ may burst from heartache. He's furious and it's all my fault. I was too careless with him.

Once I'm fully dressed and on the verge of sobbing my eyes out, Crow comes from behind the monitors. He holds out a disc to me and offers a small, empathetic smile. "He'll come around. Give him some space."

"But will he?" I ask, not buying it. It's not Crow's fault, but I'm hurt and angry at myself inside. He remains quiet. I take the offered disc and manage to make it to my car before the tears pour freely, the wound stabbing deep enough I physically ache.

I'M AN EMOTIONAL MESS AFTER BEING WITH STERLING. I CAN'T BRING MYSELF to speak to anyone about what happened either. He's never been anything but good to me, and I've ruined it. The moment he finally losses his cool around me and I think I have a chance, I screw it all up. Once he told me we could never happen, it was like a challenge set in and I'd do whatever it took to get him right where I wanted him. I thought maybe, just maybe if he were with me sexually, it'd open his eyes that I'm not just Ruins' younger sister, but a woman who wants him.

Apparently, it opened his eyes just a bit too much. Now I'm afraid I've ruined everything—our friendship and quite possibly his closeness with my brother. My family can't find out what happened or they'd freak, and I won't allow Sterling to get hurt because of something I decided to do. It's the least I can do for him in this whole mess.

I'm sorry.

I reread the text I sent a few days ago. He hasn't responded, and

I'm beginning to believe that he never will, that maybe he didn't need time to cool off and flat out hates me at this point. Everything in me is telling me to message him again or call, but I hold off. I don't know what is right or wrong to say at this point. I set my phone down and rinse my coffee cup out, setting it next to my coffeemaker for tomorrow.

I lied when I told Mom that I'm not lonely. Not having Duke around sucks, and my apartment is too quiet. I miss him. Sure, I could invite some friends over or something, but I don't like many people in my space. Maybe I should take my parents up on their offer of another dog...but that would feel like I'm dishonoring Duke's memory getting another so soon. It's hard feeling so unsure about things when a couple of months ago I thought I had everything planned out and life would be easy. There's nothing easy about any of it, and I'm beginning to learn that the hard way.

I end up texting Magnolia anyway. I don't have much to talk about if I leave Sterling out of it, and I'm definitely not wanting to bring her into the middle of it. She's my closest female friend and a good one, but sometimes I have to remind myself to keep my distance. She's not affiliated with Kings of Carnage, and while it's not a requirement or anything to be my friend, it does mean I have to be more cautious about what I say to her or bring her around. The carwash fundraiser, for example, she could've hung out and helped with me, but she had to work. Going to the club on a church day when all the members are around—not a good idea. I learned all this when I was a little girl, so it's not a big deal anymore.

Magnolia and I became friends because I was often left out of stuff, like birthday invitations or sleepovers. People have always been fearful of my dad and his club, but not me. I know what kind of man he is, and I've always been proud to say he's my father.

Magnolia, unlike others, never looked at me like a pariah, but as her best friend. I'm grateful, too, because I'm sure school would've been a fairly lonely place had I not had her by my side through it all. It sucks we're apart more with her having college, but I'm proud she's going after her dreams.

"Hey," she greets, letting herself in. I'd unlocked the door as soon as she'd texted me back saying she's stopping by. I keep forgetting to make her a copy of my key. I have one to her place, so it's only fair she has one as well. My father would be thrilled with that bit, but what he doesn't know won't hurt him.

"Hey, how was work?"

"Same as always. Bob Holland showed up, asked me for a hand job."

"No freaking way," I gasp, spinning around to face her.

She's grinning like a fool, sitting on my couch. "Kidding." Her smile drops as she takes in my swollen face. "What happened to you? Are you okay?"

I nod, deciding to just turn on my dishwasher. I could fit a few more things, but I'm not in the mood to wait for clean dishes. "I'm fine. This is from yesterday." I gesture to my puffy eyes. I've cried a few times over the last couple of days, and now I'm done with it. I've never been much of a crier, but lately, I feel like I've turned into a freaking crybaby with all the shit that's been happening. I won't beat myself up over what happened anymore so long as he won't speak to me. It's time I pull my big girl panties on and roll with it, so I'm trying.

"You were crying that bad?"

"Yeah. I pissed Sterling off and it upset me."

"I don't understand why you let him toy with your emotions. You deserve so much better." She's never understood the appeal

Sterling's held over me. She thought he was cute, but once she found out he was all I could think about, she backed off. See, that's a top-notch friend right there, one I'm never letting go of.

I shrug, not wanting to get into it anymore. "I don't want to talk about him. What are you doing tonight?" I could use her distractions. She'll have me laughing in no time. She always manages it somehow.

"Same as usual: hitting up the bonfire and drinking some beer. I may flip a few assholes off in the process. Want to join me? We can flip them off together, really leave a lasting impression."

I shrug, offering a small smile. "Who's going?"

"Doesn't matter. I'll be there, and we all know I'm the only one who counts," she retorts with a wink, and I can't help but laugh at her ridiculousness.

"Maybe for a little while. I can meet you out there."

"No way. You'll end up ditching before you make it out there. You and I both know it. You have a tendency of getting lost and ending up in your bed. You're coming with me."

"Fine," I give in with a wider smile. Thankful I have a good friend who wants to hang out with me. If only Sterling would show up and let me explain myself, but I know that'll never happen. "You need to help me figure out what to wear, and no hoe-bag shit," I comment, and she's off my couch in a flash, yanking me towards my bedroom in the next breath. This night will surely end up interesting. With Magnolia, they always do.

The only thing I know is this:
I am full of wounds and still standing on my feet.
- Nikos Kazantzakis

Sterling

I glance at Ruin. "What the fuck's going on?" I chin lift in the direction of a group of unfamiliar bikes. They're parked at one of the convenience stores on the way out of town. There's one more light then it's off to the highway. We're headed to Atlanta to do some partying and happened to be pulling into the other gas station not even a block away.

He reaches for the gas pump, but pauses and stares. "You know who they belong to?" he finally asks and moves to fill his tank.

"They don't look familiar to me. I take it Chaos hasn't mentioned anyone coming through town to you." And wearing their colors, nonetheless. Fucking ballsey, for sure. Everyone knows this is

KOC territory, and if you don't, you'll quickly find out. The Kings are quick to lay down the law and rule their territory with a heavy hand. You've got to be when there's always some asshole or another showing up to stir shit up.

He shakes his head, watching the other gas station. I haven't heard shit from my dad or around the club, for that matter. This has to be a ride-through, but they've got nerve filling up here with the potential shitstorm that could develop with it. I watch him for a beat, until my gas clicks off.

I place my pump back in its receiver and take my printed receipt, stuffing it in my jeans pocket. Closing the gas lid, I twist it tightly and I hop on my bike, moving it to point towards the road, and wait for Ruin to finish. I keep my gaze pinned on the other club, noticing the moment one gets to his bike. "Want me to text Chaos or my dad?" I can see this going downhill if they're not being respectful with their cuts already.

"Bash. He'd know if someone was coming through and whether to mention it to Chaos or not. Don't want prez to think you're trying to be a kiss ass with everything going on."

I nod, pressing out a text to my dad, thinking I should probably give North or Poe a heads-up as well. "I've never been a kiss ass," I grumble more to myself, but Ruin still catches it.

"Exactly why it may seem odd to Chaos."

"Gotcha," I reply, understanding his point of view. A rumble coming down the street momentarily distracts us as Bear pulls in next to me. I chin lift to the nomad and he returns it, looking a bit tired. "What's up, man?"

"Ready to drink a few beers and take a break for the night," he sighs, and I feel the same way in the moment. I need a breather, my feelings for Leigh, as well as shit still being a little weird with

Chaos and Ruin, have me ready to kick back and cut loose for a bit. I heard from one of the guys I used to go to school with that Leigh was at one of their bonfire parties. That stung a bit after everything that went down. I let Ruin know about it, though, and he blew up her phone all night, telling her to get home safely and if any dudes speak to her he'd mess them up. It was entertaining and worked to my advantage, as she went home alone. I saw it with my own eyes, her pulling into her parking spot and going inside by herself. I do that some nights, sit by and make sure she gets home safely.

Several motorcycles start up, my attention snapping in their direction. Ruin climbs on his bike, walking it near mine, and we both start ours as well. We sit still, idling, watching as a handful of rough-looking bikers pull onto the main strip. Rather than head for the highway, they come towards us. They're weathered and older, definitely looking like they've been through their fair share of shit to make them a nasty bunch.

I'm so busy trying to read their cuts to text my dad again who they are that I don't notice two pull weapons. One lets off a shot, and before I can blink, Bear has his drawn in return. The dude is fast. Those motherfuckers will pay for that shit. I shove my cell in my pocket, ready to ride.

Glancing to Ruin, I make sure he's okay and wasn't hit, then I take off after the dumb fuckers. I lean low and reach for my calf with my right hand, yanking my jeans up a bit to free my firearm from my ankle holster. It rests right at the top of my boot so I wear it often when riding, as it gives me easy access and is still concealed. I don't realize the others are with me, until I get close enough to return fire. Ruin shoots right after I do, and the bikes in front swerve with the echoes of our shots.

They turn right, heading deeper into town and the residential area. I'm fucked if they have any idea as to where they're headed. They can keep turning to end up behind us, unless we veer off in the opposite direction. I'm not one with a death wish normally, but I need to figure out who these fuckers are, and I want to know what spurred them on to shoot at us out of their territory while we're wearing our club colors. I'm trying to get patched. There's no way I can let them go after all this. I may only be a prospect, and Bear a nomad, but our vests still advertise which club we're affiliated with. Ruin's a fully patched member now, too, so he has the full set on his cut. I'm fairly confident Dad would call it an act of war against the club. I know Chaos, though, being prez, he always needs all the info he can get to figure out whatever decisions he needs to make. It's partially why he's a good leader, in my opinion, at least.

"Let's get the fuck outta here," Bear shouts. "We're outnumbered."

"Hell no, man," I yell back. "Gotta see who the fuck they are!"

"He's right," Ruin hollers, and we gun it as much as we can around the corner. We speed around a second turn and the bikers aren't too far ahead to get behind us…They're sitting, waiting on us, weapons drawn.

"Oh fuck, this is going to end badly," I comment to myself, but no one can hear me over the roar of our motorcycles anyhow.

I hit my brakes, turning away, and my bike tips, and the momentum has me falling to the side. I manage to get my leg out of the way before five hundred pounds of heavy black and teal metal hits the pavement and we slide. Ruin and Bear veer off in opposite directions into adjacent alleys, narrowly missing the buildings. Thankfully, I'm wearing a shirt under my cut or I'd be shredded with road rash right now. My jeans and boots help protect me as well, but I can feel my arms split open, on fire from the impact. Wetness trickles down my leg that hit the asphalt first, but my adrenaline is pumping too hard for me to pay my wounds any real attention at the moment.

Fresh shots are fired, drawing my attention. I keep my head down, finding Bear positioned at the corner of a building. He ducks behind it, then lets off some rounds, continuing to pull the riders' attention in his direction and off me. I use it to my advantage and run for my discarded gun. I slide homerun style, tearing a patch of skin from my lower back in the process. I know it has to be gone because the air hitting it feels cold and sharp. It'll hurt tomorrow, that I'm certain of. It's all good. It'll mean I'm still fucking breathing after this shit.

Getting to my feet, I hightail it for the alley I saw Ruin turn off into. A bullet hits the ground merely a foot away from my feet. "Fuck!" I shout and push myself to run harder than I ever have in my life. I plan to shoot back at these stupid fuckers when I get some cover, but I'm not trying to turn around now and die to return some fire.

The side of Ru's face comes into view as I get closer. "Hurry the fuck up, Spade!" he yells, waving me forward with one hand. His other has his gun up and pointing, but he's waiting to shoot until I'm out of the way. I pump my arms, hauling ass around the building, breathing heavily and not caring that I'm bleeding.

"Fuck!" I huff, my hands shaky with the adrenaline overload. Thinking you're going to be shot will jumble a person up inside. I don't care how much of a badass you may be, it's true.

"North, Sly, Poe, and Saint are on their way. We have to manage to hang in here until they arrive. I couldn't get ahold of anyone else," he informs and pops off a shot to offer Bear some backup.

"You had time to fucking call people?" I'm shocked. It felt like mere moment's I was laid out on the ground.

"Yeah, while you were playing Billy Badass shooting and chasing these dipshits, I was voice calling everyone my Bluetooth would allow me."

"That's what's up," I mutter, dipping into position. He shoots high and I peep around the corner staying low, letting fire rain-free. Brick and debris fly all around us as their bullets ping off various surfaces. "The cops will be here soon. This is so fucked up!"

"North will have Chaos putting a call in to his deputy contact. Don't plan on doing too much time for being shot at, bro."

I nod, releasing a tense breath. It feels like forever before the roar of a group of bikes approaching thunders over the bullets flying. The assholes in front of us must realize our club has arrived as they're not in their territory and they scramble. We manage to clip a few in random spots as they clamber onto their bikes and haul ass. I wasn't shooting to kill. I don't think any of us were, but we were aiming to hurt them and send a message.

Ruin's gaze finds mine after he glances over me, his brows furrowed and mouth in a severe frown. "Fuck, man, you're bloody everywhere."

He's worried, and for a beat I was too. The shitshow was too close to us this round and I nearly paid for it. "It's nothing serious. Just scraped up," I reassure, wanting to set him at ease. He's a good friend, always has been.

"Let's hope so. You hit the pavement hard."

I nod. I know I did. I felt it, but there was too much going on to process it at the time. "My elbow's screaming, but it'll heal. Nothing I can't handle." He holds his fist out and I bump it with mine. "Thanks for having my back."

"Always, Spade." Him calling me by my last name brings a sense of comfort after what we just went through.

North, Sly, Poe, and Saint quickly stride towards us. It looks like they left their bikes parked on the side street closest to us. "You all right?" Poe calls as we step out of our spots.

Ruin answers, "We're fine. Sterling dipped his bike, but he's only scuffed up."

Sly meets my stare, "You sure you're not shot?"

I shake my head and Ru asks, "Chaos on his way?"

North grunts out a firm, "No." He flicks his gaze between us and says, "I decided to wait until we got here to call Chaos and Bash. Regardless of them being the prez and VP, they're still your fathers. I can't have them both rolling in guns blazing, risking their necks for you guys, and I know they would in a heartbeat. I needed to handle this myself and call them in. Chaos has the club to run, and Bash is too deep with his business. I spoke to them both. They know we're here and you're fine."

I know Dad and Chaos are probably pissed about not being alerted right away, but North is right. They would've raced over here without a second thought, and that can't happen. It's probably a good thing that Ruin didn't get a hold of them first.

Sly crosses his arms over his chest and asks, "You get a club name or anything useful? Were they wearing cuts? We need info ASAP."

"I was able to get a decent look before my bike dipped. The vests had a Twisted Snakes center patch, but I missed the rest."

"Nasty fuckers. I've heard of them," North affirms. "Let's get back to the club. Chaos will want to hear everything for himself."

Saint moves to help me lift my bike. "Looks scratched and dinged up. Damn sure needs sanded and painted." I nod, gritting my teeth. I can't believe my bike is fucked up. "Get on and see if it'll start or if we need to call for Jinx's trailer."

I do so, carefully. The scrapes on my body beginning to silently scream at me. Surprisingly, my Street 750 starts right up, and I release a breath of relief. "Thank fuck," I mutter, and Saint bobs his head in agreement. "Hopefully, she rides as good as she sounds. I'm so fucking pissed I lost control like that."

"I'll stay back so we can take it slow," he offers.

"I appreciate it, man, but I need to ride her like I normally would, to see if anything's fucked up or if it's all cosmetic." I'll be putting in a call to Jupiter to see when she can fix this mess. I walk my bike towards the guys, silently stewing inside over my ruined paint. "I guess Atlanta's out of the question for the night. This fucking blows. I really need some liquor now."

Bear shakes his head. "We were just shot at and you're bummed we can't party?"

I flash him a grin. "Hey, I was looking forward to that cold beer. Can you blame me?"

Poe interrupts, "We can have a beer at the club, but first you two assholes need to update your daddies. They'll be blowing my phone up before long, if you asshats don't get to the club and show your ugly mugs."

Ruin and I both give him the bird, but he only grins, and they all head for their bikes. I walk mine with Ruin until he's back on his. "For real, Ru. I'm sorry this shit went down like it did. I fucked up."

He shrugs. "It wouldn't be our life if it were boring, you know what I mean, Spade? And you did what you needed to. Shake it off."

I nod. "Glad it happened here and not in the city. Cops would be all up our asses."

"I'm just thankful Tyra wasn't on the back of my bike today. I'd have gone ballistic if she'd been hurt."

"You better call her before she hears about it from Poe. She's stubborn, but you know she'll still worry about you."

"After we speak to our prez and VP. I don't want them on our asses, especially with how strained things have been between you and Chaos."

"Bet," I mutter, agreeing. Bear meets us in the middle of the road, and we catch up with the others, leaving in a big group. I begin to hear the faint wail of a police siren and thank my lucky stars we're on our way out of here. The deputy must've owed Chaos big, for the cops to hold off for this long. We could've ended up in jail today, and Chaos managed to save my ass from it, while Ruin and Bear had my back so I wasn't killed. This right here is exactly why the club is so damn important to me and why I'm determined to get my patch. Kings of Carnage is about true brotherhood, mutual respect for one another, and devotion to our families. Of course, it has its various businesses and hellion side where we party our asses off, but the core holds true to so much more.

We make it to the club, and it's safe to say my bike has exterior damage as well as an oil leak. Jupiter shouldn't have any issues fixing it back up for me, and knowing her, she'll have it to me in no time looking fresh. The only downfall is the custom airbrush of my spades on it is ruined. Next time I'm out through Texas, I'll have to get Dad's guy to hook me up. Regardless of my sore spots, I'm grateful. Today could've went a lot worse than it did.

Dad and Chaos are outside smoking a cigarette, already waiting on us before we make it into the parking lot. We park in the usual spots, and Dad is beside me in the next beat. He pulls me off the bike and into his embrace. If you know my dad, you know he's a hugger. He's been like that for as long as I can remember. "Are you really all right? Don't bullshit me, Sterling, I mean it."

"Scratched up from the road, but I'm not shot. You know I'm

stubborn. It'll take a helluva lot more than a dip and some stray bullets to take me out," I joke, not wanting to admit I was worried for a beat about getting shot in the back as I ran for cover.

He pulls back, firm grip on my shoulders. "Your mom is on her way. Figure you deserve to be prepared."

"Shit," I sigh, and he dips his chin, agreeing. Mom will be all over my ass about getting hurt and worrying her. Growing up, my father was protective of all of us, but that didn't mean my mom wasn't just as fierce. She has a habit of going rogue and telling us after the fact when she wants to handle something. It's no surprise that my siblings and I are so different, considering our parents tend to always do whatever the fuck they want. I suppose I come by that trait naturally from them.

"Let's get inside so you guys can fill us all in on what happened." We head for the door and he says, "Took everything me and Chaos had to stay back and wait. I don't think either one of us was expecting the club to be hit this much when you two would be getting patched in."

"It's not your fault."

"I know that, but all of us have worked hard to bring stability and a sense of normalcy to the club. We wanted our families to be involved in our club life, but not touched by the bad shit. You know what I mean?"

"Yeah. You and the brothers have always made sure we were all protected. What's happening lately, you can't control that. None of us blame any of you."

"I sure as fuck hope not." He claps my shoulder and I cringe, sore. Half my shirt's ripped off, along with some of the leather on my boots. I'm glad I had them on or I'd have been fucked up worse. I step inside and Dad curses. "You're missing some skin on your back."

I grunt. "Yeah. Fairly sure it's like that in a few places."

He hollers at the club ass to grab the bottle of alcohol, a towel, and some whiskey. If he's planning on pouring that shit on my wounds then I'm toking up too; fuck just whiskey.

"If you're pouring that on me, I'm going to go smoke first."

"Your mom will want to fuss over you, you know how she is. You guys need to give us all the details before she gets to make you scream."

He grins and I roll my eyes. That only happened one time and it wasn't something little either. I'd been out screwing around by the train tracks. I'd lost my balance, fell, slit my leg open on some broken glass, and broke my fucking arm. Mom soaked my leg in alcohol, catching me off guard, while Dad checked my arm over. Pretty sure anybody that age would've screamed, not just me. Regardless, Stryker made fun of me because he was at that dipshit age all younger brothers seem to hit a time or two growing up.

We step into church, and before anyone has a chance to sit down, Chaos demands, "Give me everything that you've got on these motherfuckers! Going after my club and my kid, way to sign your death warrant."

When your man is mad, call him 'Baby Girl' and tell him you can't talk to him when he's so emotional.
-Follow me for more relationship advice
-TikTok Meme

Sterling

I'm so fucked where my head and heart intersect, it's not even funny. I slow my speed as I cruise past the smoothie shop, neck whipping side to side like I wasn't nearly roadkill yesterday. Leigh's car's not there, and it's the only thing I was looking for. I shouldn't be riding my bike much with it still fucked up, but I can't help but choose it over my car until it goes into the shop. I make the turn to head by her apartment next, even though I damn well know it's the last place I outta be. I can still remember word for word the talk my father had with me again yesterday.

"You can't be with her, Sterling. She's not like other women around here. She'll never be club ass."

I glower in his direction at him insinuating I'd ever consider that option for Leigh. "You think I don't know that?" Part of the reason I've stayed away is because I know she's too good for what I could possibly offer her. She deserves so much more.

"Well, fuck, Sterling! Do you, son? Cause I've got my best friend pissed off at my ass for the first time in God knows how long, and it's over you and his daughter! Hell, those kids have been family to me as well, and then you go and get shit twisted up." He shakes his head, fists clenching. Dad isn't known for his patience or easy temperament. He's gotten his name from losing his shit and bashing in whatever's within reaching distance. I'm used to his temper. He's never come after me or my siblings, so it doesn't frighten me, only alerts me to his mood.

"Of course, I know she's special. Why do you think I want her?" The words leave me before I have a chance to reel them in and think. The last thing I need to do is go around spouting off that I have a hard-on for Leigh and how it feels like chewing glass to stay away from her.

He mutters, more to himself than me, "It had to be the prez's daughter, of-fucking-course. Only my kids. First Stryker constantly testing me with his fighting, and then you, neck fucking deep into club shit when you should be worried about partying and fucking off at your age. Before I know it, Sawyer will be fucking pregnant. Your wreck and run-in with the other club have me rattled enough. Don't need to add any more to it. Kids giving their old man a fucking stroke."

I snort, rolling my eyes. "I'll castrate any asshole that comes at her with his dick." I don't comment on the rest, well, because it's true. Ruin and I have always been about doing whatever we could to get into Kings and be like our fathers. Stryker's an ass always getting into shit, we all know it.

He chuckles a bit, then grows serious once more. "When I told you you'd find a good woman to change things someday, I didn't mean right now. I sure as hell wasn't nominating Leigh for that position either. You know Chaos will come for you over this? And what, Sterling, am I supposed to sit back and let him? You're my kid and as much loyalty I have for the club, my family comes first, always. Chaos knows as much. I can still remember when he met Cambri. He said brothers before all others...until her. The same happened to me when I met your momma."

I feel like utter dogshit with his words. I'm fucking everything up with this pull I have to Leigh. "I'm trying to stay away," I eventually confess. "It's harder than I thought it'd be."

He nods. "As long as you're trying to do the right thing, then I can support you. I've got your back, Ster, always. You just have to at least try." He pulls me in for a tight hug, palm hitting my back but thankfully staying clear of my road burn. "I always have you, kid. Don't forget as much."

I nod into his shoulder, not realizing I'd needed his hug and affirmation over this sensitive topic so badly. With his support, I feel stronger. I always have. It's strange how much weight a person's words can have on another.

I shake off the conversation replaying in my head from the day before and notice Leigh's car isn't at her apartment either. She's probably at her parents', which is the last place I need to be right now. Chaos would see right through me if I showed up, knowing I was looking for her. At least I know she's not alone with some douchebag and she's safe. It's enough to put me at ease, and I make the decision to head home instead of waiting her out.

I take the turn that'll bring me to my trailer. I don't live too far away from her. It wasn't planned that way or anything, just happened that we live in a small town. The ride's short and I'm pulling up to my place in no time. My car's parked under the carport where it always is, and sitting parked right behind it is Leigh's car. My brow furrows as I slow down, taking in the scene, and I drive past her car, pulling to a stop between my car and the trailer. I keep my bike tucked close so no one fucks with it.

"What are you doing here, Leigh?" I ask as soon as the rumble from my motorcycle quiets, my voice a bit gruffer than she deserves. I climb off my bike and unclip my helmet, staring anywhere but directly at her. She's standing propped against her car, arms crossed snugly over her voluptuous chest. She's wearing an expression between worry and anger. I don't like either one of those emotions on her, especially when it seems I may be the reason for them.

I stride towards the front door and impatiently ask again, "Leigh? Why are you here?" I pause, turning to momentarily meet her eyes before heading up the rickety stairs that I still haven't fixed. I can't spend too much time around her. I'm supposed to be doing the right thing here, and it doesn't help to have her showing up at my place. She needs to leave so I can keep us both out of the doghouse.

"I'm here because I'm angry!"

It's cute how she nearly sounds intimidating. I'm sure she would be to some, but I've known her for far too long to allow her tantrum to get to me. I huff out a dejected chuckle, as she has no reason to be pissed off. I'm the only one here that possesses that right. "That's rich coming from you. I'm fucking angry too," I shoot back, nostrils flaring. "You need to leave before you get me killed, before you push me too far."

Her lip wobbles and tears crest. I don't know what to do with her when she's like this. Everything in me goes on high alert and demands that I protect her. She asks, her pitch caked with emotion, "How can you joke like that? Hm?" A tear falls over her cheek.

My brows drop, confusion overtaking me. We must not be talking about being angry over the same thing. I push it aside and warn, "I'm not joking. Chaos or Ruin, hell, even my father will kill me if I go near you again. You need to get out of here." She stomps towards me, stopping to shove me with both hands. I rock, nearly losing my balance, and my arms shoot out to grab her. "The fuck, Leigh? Stop your shit already. I've had enough of it." First the fits at the studio, then her deceiving me, and now her attitude. I don't deserve this from her. Nor am I used to it. She's always been so calm and levelheaded, it's like she's gone ass backward lately.

She pounds her fist to my chest. "Ugh, you're so frustrating, Sterling Spade! I heard what happened in town. How you were shot at and rode after them, how you were nearly killed! Then you go and talk about death like it's nothing. Well, news flash, Sterling, it's something! There's enough bad in this world already..." She trails off a beat before whispering, "Don't make me picture it without you in it. I don't want to exist in a place where you don't." Tears coat her cheeks now, and it feels like something crumbles in my chest at her words.

I cup her cheeks, my thumbs moving to swipe away her tears. "Fuck, Leigh," I whisper, and then she's shooting up on her tiptoes, her mouth meeting mine. I could fight it. I should. Hell, I'm supposed to, but I don't. I want her too fucking badly to turn her touch away right now, if ever.

I hold that beautiful woman right there in front of me and take her mouth like a dying man seeking his last breath. I was so angry at her—I still am, for what she pulled at the studio—but the need to comfort her overrides anything else right now. Her hands bunch my shirt in her grip, while her mouth gives me everything I'm seeking and more.

She's so much more than I'll ever deserve, more than I can ever imagine having.

She's not mine.

She won't be, not ever.

"Leigh," I murmur against her lips, drawing back. "We can't do this. We aren't able to be together right now." I keep repeating the words silently and aloud. I need to beat them in deep so I stop this madness between us. There's no hope of the two of us ending up together in any of this. One of us, if not both, will only get hurt with it all.

"Please, Sterling, please. I need to feel you, to make sure you're okay. Show me that you're all right, that you're alive and here with me now. I want you."

Everything screams at me to walk her to her car and tell her good-bye, but I can't. I sigh, more to myself, "I hate the way I always miss you." Taking her hand, I lead her up the stairs and inside. I close and lock the door behind us and tug her to the couch. I sit, legs spread wide, not sure how to make her see that I'm okay. "Sit, Boo," I order, expecting her to plop down beside me or maybe perch on the edge since she's upset. Rather, she climbs right on my lap, thighs moving to straddle my hips. Her juicy round ass lands on my jean-clad cock, resting there, teasing me not to get hard.

My hands move to grip her sides while hers rest on the couch behind me. "What are you doing?" I ask, knowing I should just keep my damn mouth shut for once. She leans in, peppering soft kisses under each of my eyes, the tip of my nose, my chin, and then my mouth. She kisses me tenderly, drawing each of my lips between hers to suck until eventually, our tongues meet. This chick makes my head spin already, and throw in the touching and tasting and I'm a goner. My hands slide to her back, wanting to feel as much of her as I can without overdoing it and pushing her further. She's so goddamn sweet.

Her body shifts, causing me to groan. "You gotta be careful," I warn.

"Why?" She peers at me, a sweet bit of innocent curiosity staring back at me in her irises.

"'Cause, you're sitting on my lap and moving around. I'm attempting to be a gentleman here, Leigh."

Her eyes widen, a smile curling her lips. "Oh, you mean because of this?" she asks, shifting her hips forward and back, rubbing her core over my hardening length. She's a sinful tease and she damn well knows as much.

"Fuck," I whisper the curse, my hold tightening to get her to be still. "You can't do that, not when I'm not allowed to have you like I want you. You know our families don't want us to be together."

Her nose slowly nudges mine as her hips rock side to side, driving me wild. I try to think of anything to keep my dick limp, but it's no use when it comes to Leigh. "How about I do something else?" she asks, and my brows shoot to my hairline. Her hands move, and in a flash she's got her top off, tossed onto the floor behind her. It's official, this woman is trying to be the death of me.

The pad of my finger lightly trails over the globes of her breasts encased in her lacey bra. The touch is teasing, eliciting goose bumps to kiss her flesh. "Mm," she hums, reaching behind her to unclasp her bra. The elastic releases, then she's yanking it off and throwing it, baring her beautiful, lush tits. I swear she has the prettiest set of titties I've ever seen before. "I've fantasized of you for far too long to care what anyone not in this room thinks. I don't give a damn what any of them want. I want you."

Her words do something, striking a chord deep. Hearing she's thought of this for years...How have I not noticed before? Were my blinders on that much or was she simply good at hiding her true feelings from me for so long? "Magnificent," I mutter, watching as my thumb rubs circles around her silver dollar nipples and they harden to pert peaks. I'm going to taste her there and anywhere else she'll allow me to.

"Kiss me, Sterling," she commands. I eagerly obey, knowing it's wrong, but it feels right regardless.

Leaning my head to her chest, I begin by placing kisses between the valley of her breasts then explore under each globe, nipping the tender flesh and making her squirm. Eventually, I make my way to each nipple, pushing her tits together. I lavish them with my tongue and light bites. She has no idea how incredibly beautiful she is, especially in my eyes. Her hips rock forward and back, my cock growing harder with each pass of her center. The feelings are dizzyingly good. My mouth moves upwards, licking as I go until I can suck and kiss on the silky smooth flesh of her throat. I hit a hot spot as her hand flies to my hair, griping enough to give it a bit of a tug as she moans and grinds against me.

"Damn," I sigh, nearly panting and still fully clothed. "We have to stop," I repeat, knowing we're about to go past the point of no return for me. I'll be coming in her or in my pants, that much I'm sure of if we don't pump the breaks and I grab a cold shower.

"I don't want to stop. Please?" she asks sweetly, pulling back to meet my heated gaze. "I want this and I want you." Her words are the confirmation I need, and I can't get naked fast enough. Standing,

I lay her on the couch and snap my jeans open, shoving them down as I pull my cut off and fold it to the side. My shirt's removed last, tossed somewhere in the room without a second thought.

She draws in a quick breath, my name whispered brokenly, "Oh my God, Ster, you're hurt. I was just rubbing all over you, I'm so sorry. Are you okay?" She leans up, reaching to lightly graze her fingertips next to my various wounds.

Not missing a beat, I pull her body to mine, whispering against her mouth, "Fine, sugar. Don't you worry about me when I've got you like this." My cuts and bruises are long forgotten having her in my embrace.

"I don't want to injure you." She peers up at me and I grin, pressing my mouth to hers. She's so fucking sweet it damn near gives me a toothache. I kiss her until our tongues are in sync with each other, moving as one.

I push her down on the couch, and as she lays back, I break our lip lock to taste her between her thighs. Her pussy's shaved with a light-colored thin landing strip, just the way I like it. I've imagined having her this way far too many times to count, believing it'd never come true. She opens her legs wider for me and I lean in, running my nose over her tender flesh. She smells clean, like soap, and without further ado, my tongue hastily swipes up the center of her folds.

"Shit," she curses, and I take it as motivation to continue my perusal. My fingers find her entrance, teasing, while my tongue flicks her hood piercing. It has her squirming and moaning nearly immediately, making my heart pound in my chest. This woman has no clue what she does to me with her responses. The sounds that she makes drives my body wild. She consumes me in the moment. Nothing else matters but her, rules and their potential consequences be damned.

Wetness drips from her core, my mouth eagerly tasting anything she'll give me and still craving more. I don't think I'll ever have my fill where Leigh's concerned, and that thought should terrify me, yet it only prompts me to continue. Her pussy clamps around my fingers, her screams ringing my ears as she rides out her first orgasm. She's sheer perfection, pink peppering her sink, sweat dotting her brow and eyes glazed with passion. She's utterly beautiful. Never thought I'd feel like this, not with her. Hell, not with anyone, at least for a long time.

"I want to feel you inside me, Sterling," she orders, and I'm eager to obey. I move to climb between her legs and sink my length in her deep, but she's not having it. "Let me move. You take it easy."

I'm one hundred percent not going to take it easy, but I don't say as much or argue. I sit up and let her lead the way. She climbs back on my lap, positioning her sexy ass over my hips, her pussy grazing the tip of my cock. She's a fucking tease. The last time should've played as a warning how she'd taunted my cock then slammed down on it to send me over the edge. She's a goddamn vixen all wrapped up in an innocent appearing package that's sure to pack a punch.

"Condom," I manage to choke out.

"Oh shit, I don't have anything. I don't make this sort of thing a habit."

I nod, wrapping her tight in my arms, and stand. She squeals, gingerly wrapping her legs around my waist. I tote her sexy ass to my bedroom, laying her on my bed once I'm close enough.

"Are you okay?" she checks, irises flicking to my injuries.

"I'm straight. Seriously, I don't feel them right now. You're all I can think of."

She shoots me a tender smile, and I hurry to grab a few condoms from my bedside table. No way in fuck will I be done after once. I plan to have her as much as I can. If I die because of this, at least I'll go out with a bang, I suppose.

I use my teeth to rip the foil square open and move to roll the rubber over my length. "I want to taste you." She moves to lean up, and I hold my hand out towards her. She takes the condom from my fingers, laying it on her thigh. She fists my cock, licking her lips. "I've thought of this so many times."

"Oh yeah?" My lips hike into a naughty grin. She nods, dipping her head to take me into her mouth. It's soft, nearly timid at first. It reminds me of when we fucked, how she'd twirl her hips around teasingly until sinking down. She sucks my tip between her lips, rubbing her tongue back and forth across my tip. It has me seeing stars and she's barely begun. "Fuck," I breathe, watching her. She eases up on my shaft, instead lightly running her fingernails up and down my length. Combine it with her tongue and the sucking and it has me reaching for something to hold on to.

"Christ, you're trying to make me come already, aren't you?" I murmur between my grunts and groans of pleasure. My hand moves to her locks, running the silky strands between my fingers as she works me over. She releases me to dip below and rub her tongue across my piercings while rubbing her palm over my head. Wetness drips from my cock at her making me feel shit I'm not used to be experiencing. Sure, I've gotten my cock sucked plenty of times in the past, but the detail she puts in sends me to another level entirely.

"Later, sugar," I cough out, knowing I need to pull away or else I'll come and not wanting to all in the same breath. It's a struggle, but eventually I rip my hips back enough to break her sensual touch.

"I want to feel you wrapped around me too badly to just shoot off in your mouth right now. Let me make you feel good too." She nods her consent and rolls the condom on my cock. I easily push her back to lie below me on the bed. Leigh's spread out, eager, and open for whatever affection I'll offer her. The feeling's a bit addictive, if I'm being truthful. Knowing she wants me this badly to do whatever I ask of her. She's sexy as fuck.

Taking my length in my hand, I rub it through her slit, spreading her juices. I bite my lip to keep me from spilling my feelings for her in the moment. "Perfect," I comment and begin pushing inside her core. "More than perfect," I ramble on, my hips overly excited to thrust. I'm making myself be patient, though it's difficult with someone like her underneath me. I push slow and deep, relishing in the way her tight walls grip my cock so snuggly. Her hands move to my ass cheeks, gripping me tight enough to jerk me into the hilt. I grunt and she moans, her pleasure music to my ears.

Leigh's enthusiasm rivals my own and she threatens, "You either move faster or I climb on top again."

"While I love having you on top of me, I'm not trying to come in two minutes, so you'll wait your turn," I order, making her grin. She looks like she's plotting, and I already I know I don't stand a chance where she's concerned. One pop of her pussy and I'm a goner, filling this rubber with everything I've got in the moment.

She wraps her legs around me tighter, hooking her ankles together, and squeezes the muscles inside her pussy. Her walls contract and I groan, giving in. "Fine, fine. I'm too weak right now from having your lips around my cock."

My mouth dips down, kissing across her breasts and throat. I do it until her muscles relax. The moment they go lax, I slam my hips in her and repeat. She screams in bliss as the pressure hits her hood piercing repeatedly. In seconds, she's calling my name and coming around my dick. She'll learn soon enough, she's not the only one with a few tricks up their sleeve.

Imagine walking into Heaven and seeing your ex there.
Me: I see you got roaches
God: Don't start
-Pinterest Meme

Leigh

There's just something about him that makes me feel alive. Yesterday was incredible, a little rocky at first, but it didn't take long for us to have our hands on each other. I swear, I couldn't seem to touch him fast enough. I needed to feel him, and boy did I. It's safe to say I'll never get enough of Sterling, no matter how many times we're together. He was inside me half the night and I still woke up craving him this morning. I feel guilty for tricking him before with my mask, but after last night, there's not a doubt in my mind that we're meant to be together. Our chemistry with each other is undeniable.

The rumble of a bike pulling up out front has me setting my coffee down and peeping out the closest window in sight. "Shit." I jog to Sterling's room, shaking him awake.

"Mm?"

"My brother," I hiss, worrying about being here in next to nothing. My gaze scans the floor for a pair of Sterling's discarded shorts. My clothes are still in the damn living room. The door shoves open, a crack echoing as it slams into the drywall.

"The fuck?" Sterling jumps up in a flash, naked and brows low. He's pissed. I would be, too, getting woken up like that. Jesus, Ruin's overreacting just a touch.

"Ruin!" I gasp, shocked.

"You've got to be fucking shitting me." He shakes his head, glaring at Sterling. He glances over my disheveled outfit and mentions, "You know Chaos has a tracker on you?"

"Excuse me?" My mouth pops open, my hand moving to my hip as my temper flairs to life. After such a great night and peaceful morning, of course something had to come in and scramble it all up.

He nods. "He checks your phone location before he goes to bed to make sure you're safe. All of them do it. Bash has them on his kids too."

I snort. "He's so nosey. This is unbelievable!"

"You should be grateful I talked him into letting me come check on you. If he'd rolled up to see this situation, shit would be hitting the fan, and I wouldn't be able to save anyone."

Sterling sits on his bed grumbling, "And what situation is this?"

"One where my little sister was chilling at your place all night. Wanna try to convince me you weren't fuckin', 'cause he'll see through it in a goddamn heartbeat. Unbelievable. I thought you two were done flirting or whatever this is."

"This is bullshit." Sterling shakes his head and reaches for his hamper of folded clean clothes. He digs through it until he finds a pair of faded light-blue boxers and slides them on.

No longer able to old back, I burst out, "I'm a grown woman, Ru. I'm not little anymore, and who I sleep with is nobody's business but my own."

He chuckles. "Yeah, okay. First of all, you're nineteen. Second, Chaos knows everything. He always has. The brothers have tracked all of us."

"Please just go. I want to spend time with Sterling," I plead, anger making sweat dot the back of my neck. I'm fuming inside. I'm utterly in shock at all of this hitting me right now. How dare they be knee-deep in my business, family or not. No one has a right to invade my privacy as they've obviously been doing. This has gotten way out of hand, and I'm at my limit for it.

"Not happening. I'm staying until you leave or Chaos and Bash will be here next."

"Ah!" I scream in frustration. I reach for my cell and launch it at the wall. "I'm getting my own phone in my name today. You tell our father that," I demand and glance at Sterling.

His tormented stare meets mine. He whispers, "You know I can never have you, not the way I want to. You deserve better. Please leave and don't come back." His face pinches, then his irises hit the floor, no longer meeting my eyes.

I want to slam my palm against his cheek in retribution, but I refrain. I won't resort to violence right now, no matter how heartbroken and angry I am. "You know what?" I scream, past my fill of bullshit. "Fuck all of you!" I push past Ruin without a backward glance at Sterling.

I snatch up my things as I go, shoving them into my purse. I slide my feet into my plastic flip-flops and slam the door so hard the trailer seems to shake. I take it a step further, yanking out my keys. Do these guys think they can push me around as much as they want and decide my life? Well, they've got another thing coming. I won't be walked over and demanded to do anything I don't want to. It's time everyone in this town figures that out.

Gripping the key, it screeches as I trail it through the charger's glossy paint job. My brother's bike is next as I carve up his gas tank. I'm so pissed right now that I'd be leaving my mark on my father's motorcycle as well if he were here right now. They want to know how I am? What I'm doing? Well, here's a clue...I'm fucking pissed and I'm not taking anyone's shit, club member or not.

I'm not going home. Knowing my family, my mom's probably there waiting to smooth things over. I love her so much, but this isn't something her words can fix. This is the club's fault. For the first time in my life, I hate the Kings of Carnage MC.

I head for Atlanta, stopping at an ATM before I leave town so no one knows where I'm going. They've overstepped, tracking me when I'm a grown woman. Whether it's for my safety or not, it's the fact I wasn't told. It's sneaky and I don't like it one bit. I don't deserve the sort of mistrust I'm receiving, and everyone needs to realize I won't tolerate it anymore. Never again. I'm strong. I've leaned on people too much, and they've forgotten that I can stand on my two feet—alone, if necessary. I was raised that way, but it seems as if my family has forgotten as much.

I'm a hot mess, being thoroughly fucked all night, then leaving in a rush. I head for a cheap hotel. They let me keep a card on file but don't run it, thankfully, since my mom is also on the account. I hand over some cash and gratefully take the room key. The desk clerk probably thinks I'm hiding out from a crazy husband, but she doesn't know the half of it. She'd probably pee her pants if the club showed up, guns blazing, hunting me down. If my father has any hint as to where I am, it'll happen, I know it.

I take a hot shower, the water as warm as I can stand it, and use the crumbly white bar of hotel soap provided. It gives me some time to clear my head, to breathe and just exist in the constant rhythm of the shower water hitting my skin. Sometimes, the best thing to do is just pause, take everything in, and focus. I needed this moment to myself, without all the noise pounding in the back of my mind. The cheap soap leaves behind a residue feeling on my skin, but I couldn't care less. at least I'm clean again and can no longer smell Sterling's divine scent on my flesh. It was tormenting me the entire drive here.

Shutting off the now-cold water, I pat myself dry with the rough, bleach-smelling towel and wrap the scratchy material around me. I shiver as the air conditioning kicks on, momentarily freeing my thoughts, and flip through the TV for a while. Eventually, once I begin to feel like a popsicle, I put my clothes on from yesterday, already feeling dirty again.

I neatly fold Sterling's shirt and shorts, leaving them on the end of the bed. No matter how broken-hearted I am by him in the moment, I'm not foolish enough to pretend I won't sleep in them later. I will, there's no denying as much. I may be dying inside, but I'll want to smell him later.

Collecting my purse and keys, I twist my hair into a damp bun and leave to hunt down a phone store. The hotel clerk points me in the right direction, and I spend most of my day getting a new phone under my name. The rest of the time, I spend aimlessly walking around the mall that the phone store is in. I manage to pick up a few outfits on clearance to get me through, until I decide to return to my apartment. I don't know when that'll be, but one thing's for certain: I need a few days to myself. It feels reckless blowing some of my savings on nothing worth buying, but my mental heath requires it. My head's been in the clouds where my family and the club's concerned, and it's time I come out of it. My blinders are off and I'm seeing everything for exactly what it is.

I don't blame the club for my sadness and reality check. There're many good facets of the MC, I recognize as much, but it has it's flaws. Take Sterling, for example. KOC has the power to decide who he sleeps with, who he dates, who he has at his house, and who knows what else. He could be in love with me, but none of it would matter, because he's wanted that patch for as long as I can remember. Him and Ruin have talked about it nonstop since we were kids. Back then it was all one big fairytale: they'd become brothers in the club and I'd be riding away in the sunset with them both...on the back of Sterling's motorcycle. Boy was I wrong on that one. This is not some biker fairytale where dreams come true and all that jazz.

I grab some snacks while stopping to top my car off with gas and head back to the hotel. I grabbed some powdered sugar donuts and Dr. Pepper because I need some sugar overload in my life. Nothing is waiting for me there, and the loneliness of it all seems daunting. It's okay, though. I need it. I have to be able to see things clearly to remain strong. No one's pretty words and notions will sway me. I'm holding my ground.

I get to my room and order a pizza. Flipping on the TV, I wait.

And think of Sterling.

For two days I repeat the pattern, waking up to shower. I head to the mall soon after and walk around looking at stuff I care absolutely nothing about. I'm not truly shopping. I'm using the time to think and attempt to come up with a plan. I have to get my family to back off some more, and I need to figure out a way to live my life without Sterling being in the center of it. How do you move on from someone you never really had in the first place? I was fully invested with him, handing over my emotions and feelings on a silver platter, and he simply bypassed them altogether.

I finally give in and text Magnolia. She's probably worried about me, especially if the club's been around to harass her at all. I'm sure at this point they have, or at least my brother. If Magnolia didn't already know about the club, she'd probably think my family were mobsters or something. Ruin'll be doing my father's bidding, shaking down my friends and job for my location. It's too bad; they won't get it until I'm ready.

"Hey, it's Leigh," I say immediately when she answers.

"Shit! I almost ignored this thinking it was spam. Where are you? Are you okay? What happened? Tell me everything!" she peppers quietly into the phone. I can hear her shuffling around, probably moving away from customers.

"Not much to tell. I found out my family has been keeping tabs on my phone, so I took off for a while to clear my head and get some space. I love them, but I'm so angry and hurt inside over it."

"Jesus, they're like helicopter parents. I thought bikers were supposed to make you rough and tough and all that shit."

"Hardly. You know my parents. We grew up pretty normal compared to everyone else, regardless of what they may falsely believe. Anyhow, has my brother been around to ask about me?"

"No, but Sterling was here. He's coming back and he wasn't too happy."

"He only wants me around because of my family. If they weren't pressuring him, he'd care less."

She sighs and I can picture her shaking her head as she usually does when making that sound, "You're wrong. He was more turned up than usual over your absence and demanding your number. I gave him your old one, 'cause that's all I have."

"I don't want him to have this one, nor anybody right now for that matter." He can't. I'm hurting too badly right now to speak to him, and I'm not rolling over like usual. They all deserve to sweat a bit for this crap.

"He, ugh...He sorta threatened me."

"He did what?" I ask in outrage, my temper pouring into my words. Sterling's the last person I would expect to hear was threatening my closest friend. He's been acting a bit strange lately, more territorial over me at times, but still, this isn't like him. "Was he drinking? He's not usually like that," I ask, wondering if maybe that's playing a part in him threatening her, but at this rate, who knows what it could be.

"No. He was stone-cold sober. Although, I'd wager he hasn't slept much at all for the past few days. The man looked like hell, with puffy and bloodshot eyes."

"Oh my God," I murmur, and she continues.

"He said that if he doesn't get your number, he's coming back with Ruin. He promised the next step would be another brother or even Chaos after me."

"Shit," I breathe. "This has escalated far more quickly than I'd anticipated."

"Yeah, KOC's not joking around about your whereabouts and safety. To say they're concerned is an understatement."

"I only have a few people's numbers memorized. My mom, you, and Sterling, of course. I don't want to talk to him yet, but I can't handle my mom right now either. I know she'll be sad, and it'll make me feel like shit for not telling her sooner that I'm safe. I just...I can't right now."

"Shit," she curses randomly. "T-they just walked in."

"Who?" I shout.

"Sterling and Ruin. They're coming for me. Fuck a duck."

"I'm hanging up. I'll call him. Lock yourself in the bathroom if you need to." I hang up and call Sterling immediately. It rings and rings, and then rings some more. He doesn't have his voicemail set up, so it gives me a prompt and then nothing. Inhaling deeply, I exhale and try his phone again.

I feel so guilty for Magnolia having to deal with pressure from the club, but I needed to leave and I wasn't going to tell anyone where I'd gone. She may be my closest friend, but I also knew the club would hassle her eventually to get my location. To discover it was Sterling breathing down her neck does make me feel a little better. He knows she's my best friend, and I don't think he'd ever actually hurt her. Sterling may look intimidating to some, but he's not a blatantly mean person to anyone.

I use the call blocker and dial his number again. I've had it memorized for as long as he's had his phone. I was trying not to speak to him, but my curiosity's worn out over what on earth he has to say and whether it'll be on his behalf or my father's.

"Yeah," he barks into the phone before it gets a full ring in. He sounds fucking livid. Great.

"Hey, it's Leigh."

"I know who it is," he says gruffly after a beat, and I love it that his voice changes when he realizes it's me on the phone. "Where are you?"

"Why?"

"I'm comin' to get you."

"Nope. No one's bothering me. I'm on a vacation from everyone in that town."

"So you're not in town, got it. Also, how about I leave? Then I'm not one of them."

I roll my eyes, even though he can't see me. "Nope. I need some time to myself. I'm not joking, Sterling."

"Neither am I. Look, I need you to come home, okay? Do it for me."

"Why should I do anything for you? After the way things ended up, I need to stop doing things for you."

"Ouch. Look, I get it."

"Do you?"

"Yes. I was a dick, trying to stay away from you. I thought it was my only choice. I couldn't exactly be nice to you and stay away. It was too difficult."

"You hurt me," I admit softly, not wanting to be vulnerable with him anymore if he's going to keep turning me away.

"I'm so fucking sorry, Boo. Come home, baby, please. I'm begging you."

I sniffle, tears clouding my gaze. He's never called me baby before, and I really like the way it sounds coming from him. "You're begging me?"

"I am. I'll do whatever it takes, I swear it."

"Too bad I don't believe you." I hang up and cry myself to sleep.

How do you sleep at night, knowing people don't like you?
Without underwear, just in case they'd like to kiss my ass.
- libbymemes

Sterling

"Is Chaos still going crazy?" Mom asks as I close the back door. Opening the fridge, I grab a soda and take a seat at the weathered kitchen table. It's been here since I was a kid, and it brings a small sense of comfort, being here in my childhood home around family when I'm so stressed out.

I nod. "Yeah, been two days since he lost Leigh's location."

Dad's been keeping her in the loop, no doubt. Everyone in the club's been informed of Chaos looking for Leigh. He wants everyone to keep their eyes open for her car. We're all under strict instructions to call him immediately if we discover where she's at. He tried to blame me for her taking off, but Ruin had my back. He stood up to his father, telling him it was the phone tracking that made Leigh lose it and take off. Not that I can blame her for it. I'd be pissed finding out my family had been keeping tabs like that on me as well. Unlike her, I've known about the phone tracker since I first got mine. Dad was upfront with me. I thought everyone knew, but obviously that's not the case, and I'd forgotten about them until this mess blew up.

"Jesus, I can only imagine how worried he and Cambri must be. We're all praying she returns home safely."

"She's an adult," I throw in, even though I've been doing nothing but worrying and driving around looking for her. I had to take my bike in, the oil leak getting worse, and I've been too busy with club shit to really work on it. Besides, I know Jupiter needs the money right now.

"We all know that, love, but she's also the MC president's daughter. Do you realize what kind of danger she could be in if the wrong person found out she's gone without anyone running protection? It's one of the many reasons why Cambri and I stuck so close together raising you kids along with Chaos' sister. We never knew what could be lurking, and having each experienced our personal touch with danger, it kept us vigilant."

"I thought it was just because you guys were good friends." Her comment doesn't make my unease lift at all. If anything, it doubles down, making my gut churn with worry.

"Well, of course. I've known her for about twenty-two years now. Her and the club's very dear to me. The same goes for most of the other wives as well. We've always stuck together, one big tight-knit group. It kept us all safe, happy, and we knew we could trust each other."

I release a sigh, my brow bunched, and fingers massaging my

temples. "I don't know what else to do to help. I'm at a loss, and I hate to admit as much," I confess. "Aspen's had the dancers trying to find out information from the customers at Centerfolds. As well as Michaela quietly asking the regulars down at the Pub. I've been checking in on each place between the smoothie shop and her friend Magnolia. Have you heard anything at the diner?"

Dad helped Mom buy the tiny restaurant back when Sawyer was around six and she'd become busy with school. Mom was sick of only working part-time, and when the diner became available, it was a done deal before anyone in town knew the building was for sale.

"You care for her," she notes, her eyes empathetic. I know she can tell how tired and upset I appear. I've tried keeping it locked down, but the last time I glanced in the mirror, even I could see that I'm not hiding it well.

"More than you could imagine."

She flashes me a soft smile, reaching out to squeeze my forearm. "I feel like you've talked to everyone about this but me," Mom says, leaving no room for me to slide my way out of sharing. "Tell me what's been going on with you, what's on your mind."

After a beat, I release a tense breath and admit, "I want to be with Leigh, but it's forbidden."

"By whom?"

I shouldn't say anything, but our families are close, and I don't like keeping stuff away from my mom if I don't have to. "Chaos, and then Dad, and probably Ruin...hell, the entire club, I'd bet, since Chaos isn't on board."

"Oh no." She shakes her head, immediately disagreeing. "No, my son, everyone isn't against it. You go talk to her momma, she'll tell you as much."

"Cambri?"

She nods. "She asked me a while back if I thought you and Leigh ever had a chance. She loves you, Sterling, and I'd bet she'd stand up to Chaos on your behalf and help him see reason."

"Seriously? But that's her ol' man, the prez."

"She's his wife and Leigh's momma. She has every right to have a say in the matter too. Chaos respects that. He's a good man, as is your father. But, Sterling, you need to realize a few things. The club is a huge part of your father's life. It's been that way since I first met him, and I've always respected that part of him. I kept out of his business and supported him, but that doesn't mean the club is your life as well. I know it means a lot to you, that the brother's approval and acceptance weigh heavy. Ruin is patched now, and he's your best friend, so, naturally, you want to be beside him through it. However, I'll say it again—you owe the club nothing."

I get up to throw the soda can away and splash some water on my face. My eyes burn, but I refuse to rest until I figure out where she is.

Mom stands, coming to lean against the counter, and continues, "You aren't a member yet, nor do you have to be if you changed your mind. Club life is a choice, one you have to be ready for. You can't let the club choose your love life on top of everything else. You'll grow to resent it. If you want Leigh, genuinely desire her like no other...then you do not hold back. You go for it with everything you've got, because you only live once, son, then life is over. You think long and hard about the future you want. If you decide on both, you can have that too."

I dry my hands and face with a paper towel, turning towards her. I meet her stare, taking in everything she's saying. Is it true? Can I have both?

She reaches out to me again and says, "Step up and be the man I know you are. If your father has anything to say, you send him my way. I'll take on Sebastian, as I always have when I've needed him to truly hear me. Talk to Cambri if you're unsure, and remember, Ruin loves you. He's your best friend and brother. Family forgives, and he will too."

I'm not going to try to lie, I'm choked up at what Mom said. I needed to hear it all so damn bad, and she laid it out for me. "Love you, Mom," I say. It's all I can manage to get out right now.

She pulls me in for a hug, and even dwarfing her, she still feels like she could take on the world for her family. "Love you too, Sterling. Forever."

I leave and drive by Leigh's work again. She's still not around, and the girl working there, Shauna, claims to know nothing. I don't buy it. Leigh's responsible. She's always been that way when it comes to her job, so I know they must know something. I guess she could call and pretend to be sick. The owner would probably buy it in a heartbeat, since Leigh never shams off like that. Fuck. This has got to be really bad if Leigh's not showing up for her shifts. I veer off, heading for Magnolia's job next. She's there, thankfully, but doesn't look too pleased to see me. Although, she never does. She's probably sick of dodging the club, but I know she must know something where Leigh's concerned, no matter how small the detail may be.

"Magnolia," I bark, demanding she gives me her attention. It works and she comes my way, glowering.

"What do you want?"

My hands raise in surrender. "Easy. I'm just stopping by to see if you've spoken to Leigh since yesterday."

"Why do you care? Aren't you done messing with her heart by

now? She called like you wanted her to."

My hands fall, fingers curling into fists. "I'm not messing with her, I swear it."

She snorts. "Sure. She may buy into your bullshit, but I don't."

"Look, none of that matters right now. She's missing and we're worried. I know damn well you've spoken to her since she called me yesterday."

Her eyes dart to the side but she shakes her head. "I have no idea what you're talking about."

"Right. Well, let me enlighten you on something you seem to be missing. If you don't talk to me, tell me what you know, you'll have Chaos questioning you. Or how about Bash? You've heard how my dad loses his shit and flies off at the handle, right? Pick your battles, Magnolia. You either come at me with your attitude and help me out, or you face the club breathing down your back. I can only warn you of the consequences so many times before the big dogs come for you." I lean in, my mouth close to her ear as I murmur, "Don't worry, I'll make sure to dig the hole deep enough so strays won't try to get to your body."

She draws in a quick breath, my words sinking in. She swallows and says, "Let me see if I can talk her into contacting you again, but I don't know. You've really hurt her this time, and not just you, her family too."

"Give me her number. Surely, you have it by now," I demand.

"I still don't have it."

"Bullshit," I counter, shaking my head. "I know you've spoken to her."

"I swear to God. I did hear from her this morning, okay? She's fine, but the number came up as private like before. I'm not lying to you. Trust me, I don't want to die."

"You better hope so," I cruelly breathe the threat. "'Cause she's the only thing keeping me from stealing your last heartbeat." I twist on my heel, calling behind me, "I'll be back tonight. You better have something for me, or you'll be dealing with the consequences." She says nothing, but she doesn't need to. I've gotten my point across, and that's all that matters. Climbing back into my Charger, I shoot a text to Dad, letting him know I stopped by to speak to Magnolia and she's going to try to reach Leigh again. I get a reply immediately.

Dad: Does she know anything?

Me: I'm stopping back by later. She's going to try to get a number for me by then.

I know he'll relay the message to Chaos and Cambri. It's not what anyone wants to hear, but at least it's something. I'm not just sitting around twiddling my fucking thumbs until I lose my mind. I swear if anything happens to her during all of this, I'll never forgive myself. Mom is right, all I've done is waste time. I could've been with Leigh this entire time, rather than fighting the natural pull I feel towards her. If I'd been serious about it from the beginning and stuck with it, there's a possibility of our families having accepted us together by now. Rather, I've fucked off, yo-yoing back and forth with her feelings while showing everyone else she wasn't priority enough for me to fight for.

No more. I'm done standing down when it comes to my life. The club will rule nearly everything I do, and I'm okay with that, I welcome it, in fact. However, I will not give KOC the power to decide my fate where love's concerned. There has to be more than the club for me, and that more is Leigh. I don't have a doubt in my mind, she'd make one helluva an ol' lady when the time comes and she's ready for it. Chaos may not've wanted her to end up with a brother, but he should be able to recognize that I'd be fiercely protective of her. Not only that but she'd be happy, and this is a way to keep her even closer to the club. She wouldn't just be the princess or club brat anymore; she'd be a member's ol' lady. Well, she would if I manage to make it that far. It was never an issue I gave thought to in the past, but shit's went on and damn near done a one-eighty, tossing life up in the air for me.

I hit up the club next. It's like a time bomb is ready to go off. The brothers are outside smoking, staring at me as I park and climb out of the car. I need to speak to Cambri about Leigh, but now's certainly not the time. Tension is too high, and if I bring up my feelings for Leigh, Chaos may lose it and finish me off at this point.

Bash heads for me, stopping to rest his hand on my shoulder. He flexes his grip. "You did good, son. I've known my brother for many years, and I can tell your words eased the burden resting on his shoulders. Someday, you'll understand when you have some kids of your own. Their safety and happiness is everything."

"My happiness?" I pause to ask.

He nods. "Of course."

"And if I said I was done fighting this thing between me and Leigh?"

He sighs. "Not this again, Sterling. Haven't you learned your lesson by now? Look where we are right now, Christ."

"Only thing I learned is that I've been wasting time. I've been hurting someone I love and it's making me miserable inside. I want the club more than I can express, but I've come to realize that I want Leigh, too, more than my patch. I know it's supposed to be brothers above all others, but not when it comes to Leigh. If that makes everybody hate me or be disappointed in me, so be it. It'll crush me, but it's a burden I'll bear for her. I'm done seeing her cry because I turn her away. I only want to make her smile, to make her happy. I love her, Dad, I do."

His gaze is trained behind me and I know there must be someone at my back. A heavy hand clamps down on my opposite shoulder, and without looking, I know it's Chaos. He's heard everything I said, and my father didn't even attempt to stop me from saying it. Rather, he says, "I was wondering how long it'd take for you to stand your ground."

"Same here," Chaos practically growls.

I toss my hands up, exasperated. "Fucking beat me, bury me, whatever. I'm done keeping my feelings for her suppressed." Chaos comes to stand beside me, Dad still directly across. Both of them peer at me, staring so hard, it's like they can see inside me or something. "What?"

Dad says, "You realize that there isn't any going backward with her, right? Our families are forever linked, and if you two fuck up whatever you've got, it'll mess with all of us. We can't have it. You have to be one hundred percent in with her. No turning back."

"I'm in," I reply immediately.

Chaos scratches his beard, staring me down, his gaze hard. "First off, we vote on your patch. Not having any daughter of mine with a fucking prospect."

I nod, scared to swallow or even breathe and fuck the moment up. "I'll do anything."

"You get my daughter to come home. I don't care what it takes. If she wants to be with you badly enough, I'll give in. For her."

My head jerks in another nod, wishing Leigh would stop being stubborn and call me already so we can fix this. "I'll go back to Magnolia and wait by her until Leigh calls back."

"You do that. My girl comes home, we vote on your patch."

"Thank you."

Dad grunts, "Don't thank him yet. Your ass is still a prospect right now."

Chaos gestures to Ru. "Ruin, ride with Sterling. I want you with him to add more pressure on Magnolia, like yesterday."

He obeys, fist bumping me as he passes. He hops into the passenger side, and I promise to text with any update. I climb in the beast of a car, her engine rumbling loudly as I pull out of the club parking lot and gun it. I don't care where Leigh is; the moment I have a lock on her whereabouts, I'm gone. I'll stuff her in my damn trunk if I have to. Whatever it takes, she's coming back home where she can finally be mine.

Never let your storm get your kids wet.

-Unknown

Leigh

Inhaling deeply, I exhale and call his phone again. I can't have any of them hurting Magnolia because of my absence. I'll never forgive myself for it, or them, for that matter.

"Yeah?" he barks again, sounding pissed off at the world. It seems to be his go-to mood right now. I wonder if I'm to blame for that?

"Sterling, it's me."

"Boo?" He comes off relieved. "That you...you all right?"

"I'm fine. Seriously, you guys are being ridiculous, and leave Magnolia alone. You've scared her enough. It's not making me want to come home any sooner."

"Your brothers grilling her again, right now," he admits.

"Well, stop him, please."

"Nope. I won't be stopping anything until I have your digits and know where the fuck you are."

"Don't act like you care."

"But I do."

"Bullshit," I argue, ready to hang up on him like I did yesterday. I don't care how good his voice sounds, I'm still mad at him and everyone else. "Your loyalty belongs to the club, to my father and Bash. I finally understand that, and I'm learning to make peace with it. You have them, and with some time, I'll have someone that wants me more than anything else. You all need to leave me alone, let my heart heal so I can move on with my life, and from you."

"What the fuck, Leigh? So I don't get any say in this? Do my feelings mean nothing in all this mess? I feel like I just got a taste of you and you're already making me brush the flavor away."

"That's rich coming from you, Sterling. I've followed you around like a pathetic puppy since I was a little girl. I worshiped the ground you walked on, always waiting off to the side while you flew through women and filmed porn with whores. I stood strong, knowing someday our families would finally be joined, that I'd be on the back of your bike with the title of ol' lady. I offered you my whole world...I ripped my heart out, bloody and pumping, willing to give it all for you."

He coughs, his voice a bit strangled as he curses, "Fuck. Christ, Leigh. How you gonna say some shit like this when you're not in front of me? How am I supposed to pull you to me right now? To hold you and tell you I'm done fucking up, I'm ready to fight for you? You're calling it quits, and I'm strapping up, ready to go to war for you, baby. Come home. Let me make this better and help you heal from my fuck-up."

"You can't say stuff like that, Sterling. It'll completely ruin me. It's already hard enough to face what needs to be done to move forward."

"Nah, fuck that. You're mine, Boo, and you always will be. I see it now, and I'm not letting you go. If I have to be out here grinding, working for your forgiveness and your heart again, I'm gonna do it. You just watch me, beautiful. You won't see anybody but me, I'll make damn sure of it."

Tears pour out of my eyes, as the words I've always wanted to hear from him finally leave his mouth. Is it too little, too late though? Can I give him my soul again and trust he won't crush me all over? I'm scared now, about him and the future. "My father will never allow it, no matter how badly I want it," I sob into the phone, no longer holding my emotions at bay. I love this man and I always have.

"Baby. Tell me where you are."

With a defeated huff, I rattle out the hotel I've been holed up in Atlanta.

"Text me them digits, Boo. I'm dropping your brother off then I'm coming for you. We got some shit to handle."

"I don't want anyone else coming with you. I'm not ready to speak to my family."

"I won't say anything until after I drop Ruin off."

"I know my family, they'll come here regardless of what you say."

"No, I'll tell them I'm going to check out a place I think you're at. We'll talk, and then I'll let them know you're fine and I've seen you with my own two eyes."

I give in because I want to see him. I should keep my distance, but I simply can't bear it when there's the possibility out there that we could finally be together in some way.

There's a knock at my hotel door about two hours later, and I know it's him. The real question is if he listened to my wishes and came alone or if there's a mob of bikers waiting to escort me back home. Glancing through the peephole, I take Sterling in. He's wearing his cut, white T-shirt, and jeans. He's got his hands halfway into his pockets as he glances around the hallway, casing the place.

I open the door and his head tilts, taking in my swollen face and disheveled appearance. "Babe," he mutters softly. He pulls me into his strong, warm embrace and tucks us inside the room. "Jesus, woman, this place is kinda a shithole. I can't believe nobody fucked with you."

I shrug, my body at ease against his frame. He feels like home to me, and his smell pulls me in deeper. "I knew no one would give me a second thought here."

"I swear you're blind looking in that mirror. You're gorgeous, even when you think you're a mess." I pull back enough to peer up at him. His hands move to cup my cheeks, and he leans in to touch his lips to mine. It's tender, slow, and almost timid as he tastes my mouth after what feels like has been forever. I've missed him badly, far worse than I realized, until I opened that door to let him in.

"Did anyone follow you?"

He shakes his head. "I told Dad where I'd be. He told me to text to let him know you're okay, and they'll leave us alone for a few hours. They want you to come home, though. Everyone's been worried sick, not just your parents. The entire club's been out looking for you."

"I'm sorry. I just couldn't handle everything anymore. I needed to get away."

"I get it, more than you realize." He leads me to the bed, and we both sit, facing each other. "You scared me. With the way things ended up, and then you disappearing...I didn't know what to do or how to even act. I can't lose you, Leigh. Not ever again. You have to promise me."

"I've always loved you," I admit softly, and he reaches for my hand, entwining our fingers. "I don't know how to change the club's decision on us, and I know how much their opinions mean to you."

He grabs for my other hand as well and says, "Not as much as you. You mean more to me than all of it."

I meet his stare. "Since when?"

"I suppose always...It just took me a little while to realize it. I'm sorry I hurt you. It's the last thing I've ever wanted to do where you're concerned."

"And what about my father and my brother? I don't want them to hurt you because of me."

He leans towards me, pushing until I lie down, and he's hovering over me. Flashing a grin, he hums, "Mm. Chaos said I can have you if I bring you home."

My eyes widen, a quick gasp falling from my lips. "He did?"

He nods, pressing a swift peck to my lips, then dipping into the crook of my neck to suck the tender flesh. "Yeah, Boo. You're all mine. You ride back with me, and I'll send up someone to get your car. I'm not ever letting you go again."

"That's a pretty big promise, even for you, Sterling Spade."

"Good thing I'm stubborn as fuck, baby." He pushes the oversized sweater I found on clearance off my shoulder to continue his blissful assault. He murmurs against my skin, "I meant what

I said to you on the phone. I'm not backing down anymore. You want me, you're gonna get me full force. Hope you're ready for what you're getting."

"I've been ready and waiting," I confess, moving to peel his cut free and then his T-shirt off. He's gorgeous like this, in only his jeans, his attention trained solely on me.

"You gonna let me have you? All of you? Once we start this, there's no stopping it." He pulls back to remove my shirt and then moves for my chest. His tongue toys with my nipples, making me squirm. One hand locks on my hip, holding me in place as he drives me wild, sucking my breasts and grinding his hardness against my core.

"Yes. Take everything," I reply breathlessly.

He pushes his jeans down then tugs my tiny sleep shorts free. My legs spread wide, his length resting in the apex of my thighs. My fingers trail over his back, my nails scoring his flesh, ready to rip him apart if he doesn't sink inside me soon. "You want this? *Really* want this?" he asks again, making sure. He's giving me the opportunity to change my mind and back out, but in the same breath, I don't think he'd allow it. In the end, he'd still be taking me home as his, no matter how hard I try to fight it.

"I do," I confirm, and he slides his cock through my slit, spreading the wetness. In the next dip of his hips, his tip finds my opening, and then he's pushing inside. The first thrust is slow but deep, both of us groaning in relief.

"This is where I belong," he admits, and I couldn't agree more.

"Yes. You and me, Sterling."

"That's right, Boo. Me and you from now on. I swear it."

My lip trembles as emotions hit me tenfold. I'm so happy right this very moment, and I never want to forget this feeling. My hands find his back, palms flat, fingers spread, attempting to feel every possible inch of him I can at once. Leaning up, I press kisses on his shoulder, leading up his throat to his ear. I lightly suck his earlobe between my lips and whisper, "Always."

My hands rub up and down his back, moving over his flesh in a powerful motion. I'm careful to avoid his injuries as I pull him to me with each upward motion, wanting him to remain rooted deep. I could just lay like this for hours, him warming me with his weight and presence, his length filling me, words serenading my soul. It's almost too perfect, like a dream. My puffy face and tired eyes reassure me that this is every bit real, that Sterling's here with me, saying the things I've longed to hear for so long.

His hand scales down my side, tenderly brushing over my breast, abdomen, hip, and then thigh. He grips my upper thigh, pulling it up and close to his body. It shifts our position a bit, and I swear I feel him in my belly the next time he sinks down. My eyes roll heavenward, relishing in how he fills me so completely. "Harder," I beg.

"Nope. I'm going to take my time and stare at you, Leigh. I need to know you're okay. I don't think you realize what it did to me inside when I couldn't find you, when I didn't know if you were safe."

My hand goes to his scruffy cheek. I doubt he's shaved since I've left. He's as much of a mess as I've been. "You're here now. You know I'm okay."

He slides in and out, his forehead coming to rest against mine, eyes closed. He releases a sigh, the tightness in his shoulders easing up a bit. "I'm not losing you again. No way," he declares, moving his hand under my other thigh. He positions it over his shoulder and we feel so incredibly close, it's extremely intimate, having him in all of my space like this.

His groin strokes my clit with every move, my piercing heightening each touch to the point it's nearly too much. The ridges from his piercings are more prominent without a condom and it feels amazing. I should be concerned he's bareback, but I can't bring myself to care right now. I love this man, I always have, and I know he would never hurt me in that type of way.

"You feel so good," I softly confess, pulling his lower lip between mine to suck. I release it, copying the move with his upper, before nipping along his scruffy jaw. My face will be pink tomorrow from his kisses, but I'll relish in the soreness. It'll be a pleasant reminder of right now, and I never want to leave this moment. It's everything with him.

"So do you, Boo, more than you know. I swear this pussy was made for my cock, so tight and fluffy." He shivers as a burst of sensation hits him. "Fuck," he curses, and his words bring a smirk to my lips. He's home, that's why it feels so good and natural. I hope he realizes as much. He belongs with me, his cock inside me, there's no doubt in my mind.

"I'm close," I admit.

"Mm," he groans, tucking his face into my neck. His warm breath mixed with the tender licks and kisses make my head spin. My pussy clenches as the first bit of orgasm begins to spiral, shooting from my breasts to my curling toes. "That's it, baby, squeeze my cock."

I couldn't hold back if I tried. My core pulses, flexing and releasing as wetness escapes around his length. "Sterling," I breathe his name with my orgasm, and it sets him off. He throbs, warmness flooding my center as his release splatters my walls, coating me in his essence.

I've never felt more complete in my life.

A female never forgets how a man treats
her during a time she needs his support most.
- Pinterest Truth

Sterling

"You ready to do this?" I glance at Leigh. she's worried, I can see it all over her face. Reaching over, I take her hand in mine, wanting to offer her some comfort. I hate it that she's feeling antsy inside, and there's nothing I can do to change it for her. I'm actually feeling much better today, so I know she's fine; I got some time with her and a bit of sleep.

She nods. "I had time to think about things. I need to apologize for leaving abruptly, but also tell them to back off. I love my family, but I deserve the same respect I show them."

She's been calmer than I anticipated. I figured she'd be jumpy on the ride back to the club, but she's been quiet, lost in her head.

We took the rest of the day yesterday to talk and explore each other. I let Ruin and Dad know she was with me and safe so everyone backed off and we had a quiet night spent together, wrapped in each other's arms. We'd showered this morning and ate some breakfast, then I knew it was time to come back down to reality. Chaos said he'd lay off if I brought his daughter back home, and I one hundred percent plan to see it through. I'm not letting this gorgeous woman slip through my fingers again.

Taking the turnoff to the clubhouse, I follow the short road and eventually park near the prospects' bikes. It grows even quieter as I cut the engine and the rumble disappears. "Come on, Boo," I coax. "I've got you, remember? I'll be beside you through this, as much as you want me to."

The door to the clubhouse flies open and out pours the cavalry. Chaos leads the pack, closely followed by Cambri, Ruin, Dad, Mom, Stryker, and Sawyer. So much for not overwhelming Leigh. I suppose she's used to it, though, with everyone all up in each other's business around here. We get out, and then Leigh's being passed to each of them. Everyone wants to hug her and tell her they're happy she's okay. I am too. I thought I was going to lose my mind not knowing where she was. She's safe and with me now, so it's all that matters at the moment.

Chaos makes his way to me after he's held his daughter tightly and seen for himself she's more than fine. "You kept your word."

"Of course. I'll always protect her."

"And make her happy?"

"I'll damn sure do what I can to keep her happy. I love your daughter, Prez."

"Then it's time for church." He turns to Dad. "Bash, time for church."

Dad nods, pulling his cell free. “I’ll text everyone.” He immediately shoots off the text in our group chat, making mine, Ruin’s, and Chaos’s phones chime with the alert.

Leigh’s gaze meets mine and I gesture to the club. “I’ve got church. You straight?”

Cambri cuts in, stepping to me. She tucks her hand in my elbow. “Come on, Sterling. We’ll all go inside with you guys.”

“All right.”

She beams up at me, allowing Leigh to have a moment with Ruin. I’m sure he’s peppering her with questions about where she’s been. My siblings follow at the back, used to club life. “Thank you for bringing my girl home.”

“Of course.”

She gives my arm a light squeeze. “You were always meant to be her protector. I’m glad you two have finally found each other the way I’ve known you were meant to.”

“You’re not angry about it?” I leave out the part about Chaos being on the verge of killing me for going after their daughter. He didn’t ever have to mention the words; I could see it written in his expression. If I’d gone after her right away, this situation would’ve ended much differently.

Shaking her head, she flashes me an exasperated glance. “I’ve always thought of you as a son, and this only solidifies that notion even more. Just be good to my daughter.”

“You have my word.”

“All right, lover boy, go to church. I have a feeling this session is about you.” She grins, making me scrunch my forehead with confusion. Church is for me? Before I can say anything else, Chaos is kissing her like his life depends on it, and Dad’s clapping me on the back, walking me to church.

The brothers make their way around the table, sitting in their usual spots. I stand against the wall, behind my father's place. He's my sponsor, so this is where I belong in this room. The other prospects move into place, Mako behind Jinx, Saint behind Sly, and Crow behind North. Bear sits off to the side since he's a nomad hanging around the club to help out a bit.

"Now that my daughter's been safely brought home, we have a few matters to discuss," Chaos begins once everyone's settled into their places. "Bash." He nods to Dad.

"As y'all know, I've taken Sterling under my wing the past few years and have taught him about an important source of the club's income." The brothers nod, keeping him talking. "Chaos has given his vote to patch Sterling a full member and as his sponsor, I agree with our prez. Sterling has helped bring in a lot of deals and is trustworthy. He's loyal to the Kings of Carnage, to all of us, and it's time to put it to a vote. I'm nominating he receive his patch today."

Chaos stares at me a beat before saying, "Sterling has my vote." Dad speaks up next, confirming, then the rest of the table follows suit. My chest is racing, my heart beating so fast it's like running laps. I trusted Chaos' word, but I didn't think they'd vote on it right now. I'm thrilled, don't get me wrong, just a bit overwhelmed—in a good way.

Church grabs a fresh patch from one of the safes and hands it over to my dad. Ruin gets up from his place and scoots another chair next to his. I'm the lowest on the totem pole, but I couldn't give a fuck. I'm a member, a fucking King, and that's all that matters in the moment. I take the patch, thanking everyone, and sit in the vacant chair. Bear leans over, slapping me on the back in congratulations. He knows this has been a huge priority of mine and it means a great deal.

"All right," Chaos grumbles after a beat, and we all quiet down again. "We still have this Twisted Snakes issue to discuss. I've been in contact with a few clubs since the shit went down in town, and they've had the same bullshit happen to them as well."

Jinx huffs. "The fuck? They trying to go to war?"

Chaos shrugs, "Truth is, none of us know what the fuck those pussies are after. Several members of other clubs have been shot. They've been scouting for more information like us."

Dad speaks up, "It's random. It's fucking everyone up. No one is expecting it, so no one is reacting quick enough."

Sly agrees. "And innocents can get caught in the crossfire. It's basically a fucking drive-by. God forbid they'd been by the Pub or the truck stop. Could you imagine how many people could've been shot if they were?"

North mentions, "The girls at Centerfolds haven't heard anything either, and usually they catch a lot of shit from Johns passing through town. So not only are the Snakes hitting, but they're doing so quietly."

Bear offers, "May be a good time to call on some more Nomads. Get a traveling group together, chase them down out in the middle of nowhere to take care of business."

Chaos' head bobs, "Yes, that's exactly what we need to be considering."

It grows quiet as everyone contemplates options, so I say, "I'll go when my bike's out of the shop. Should have it back this week or so, then I can be one to volunteer."

"No," Dad grunts immediately.

Chaos backs him up, "He's right. It's too risky. We don't know fuck all about this other club's usual whereabouts. I like Bear's suggestion of a nomad group. I can make some more calls, see if there's some boys wanting in on it to hunt these bastards out on the open road. The nomads will know the lay of the land—depending on where it is—better than we would. We're familiar with here and the surrounding areas. If we stick to where we know, we're less likely to die while picking them off should they come back through. We need to protect this town while getting our payback."

"And if we go to war?" North inquires.

"You know that's last resort," Dad says while glancing around the table. "We have our families to think of. We're not all young kids anymore with shit to fall back on."

Chaos grunts, "Agreed. For now we do some more digging and keep our eyes peeled. I'll reach out to some other charters and see about a nomad group. In the meantime, stay on your guard. If they roll through, pop it in the group chat immediately. If you receive the text from anyone, drop whatever the fuck you're doing and go in for backup. I want these motherfuckers dead if they roll through our territory again. We'll send a message either way we end up going about this."

Me being fully patched now means the Twisted Snakes shot at two patched members, as well as a nomad. It's a big statement for an out-of-town club to make. It usually ends in significant blowback and at times a turf war. Chaos doesn't want their turf, but with what went down, he may offer it to another KOC charter in trade for something he does want. Nashville KOC is closer to the Twisted Snakes MC, so they may be interested in this as well.

Chaos calls an end to church, pausing beside me long enough to remind, "You have my daughter to protect now. Don't die before she has a chance to be happy with you or I'll dig your ass up and shoot you myself."

My hands raise, palms out. "Don't have to tell me twice." And I mean it. Leigh is my priority, aside from Kings of Carnage, and she always will be. I thought I was going to lose my shit not knowing where she was for a few days, and I never want to face that feeling again.

"Shots!" Ruin shouts as we head out of church and he scoops Tyra into his arms. Those two have gotten hot and heavy and I'm happy for them both.

I seek out Leigh immediately, and I won't lie, it feels sweet having her waiting for me. It's also damn good finally having my member patch. A sense of belonging washes over me. I've always wanted to be a part of this club with my best friend and here we are, fully patched members for life. "You got patched?" she asks, brows raised. It looks like she was crying a bit, but seems to be fine now.

"Yeah, they just voted me in," I murmur, reaching out to grip her hip. I pull her in closer.

She beams. "Congrats. I'm so happy for you."

"For us," I lean down, murmuring against her lips. "We're a team now, remember?"

"I could never forget, nor would I want to." She pushes up on her tip-toes, pressing her mouth to mine. I don't take it as deeply as I want, respecting her father. I'll give him a little more time to warm up to me and Leigh being a couple. It doesn't mean I won't be affectionate towards her, but I'll definitely be respectful about it.

"You're not upset being deeper into club life?"

She holds me tightly, laying her head to my chest. "Of course not. I love the club. I enjoy all of it. My issues weren't with KOC. It was with not having privacy and the option to make my own choices." I nod, peppering a kiss to the top of her head.

"Thanks, brother," I say to Ruin as he hands a shot to me. I can finally call him brother and it has a new meaning behind it.

"Uh, how about me, assface?" Leigh scolds and Ru grins.

"I spoke to your boss. You have to work in an hour."

"Shit!" She pulls out of my hold. "Thanks for reminding me. I've been stuck in a bubble since last night and didn't realize it's already Tuesday."

I tap my glass to Ruin's and hold it up. Everyone around me holds theirs in the air as well. "To Sterling," they cheer in unison, and I toss the tequila back.

"Can you give me a ride before you drink too much?"

"Yeah, I can drop you off, and I'll make sure you have your car by the time you get off."

"Thank you." she offers me a grateful smile and I can't hold back from kissing her again. She's so fucking sweet.

Cambri interrupts, "How about I take you now so you can change and Sterling can celebrate with his brothers."

"I don't mind," I say immediately, not wanting Leigh to ever think I'd shove her off to party.

"You've earned it," Cambri says. "Besides, it'll give me a chance to catch up some more with my daughter."

I glance to Leigh and she nods. She gives me another kiss and promises to see me after work. I have a feeling she'll be picking my ass up if Ruin has any say in the matter. Dad comes over next, hands loaded with Kamikaze shots, since he's a vodka drinker, and I know damn well it's going to be a crazy, loud night. One I'll hopefully never forget.

The wise man said:
Do not take revenge, the rotten fruits will fall by themselves.
- Pinterest Meme

Sterling

A few weeks later, Ruin hurries towards me as soon as I enter the club. "What's up?" I greet, instantly alert.

"Chaos got a hit on the Twisted Snakes' location."

"No shit? They close?" I want to catch them this round while being prepared. I don't take kindly to being shot at. We've been sitting back, collecting whatever we can on their club, and I think we're all feeling a bit better because of it. Not only that, but it's given us time to plan on how to handle it.

"That's the thing, brother, remember how prez was saying the Snakes were pulling the same with other clubs?"

I nod.

"They hit Texas, came across some Oath Keeper's MC Nomads."

My mouth drops open. That's the same club my father works with. One of them had airbrushed our tanks a while back. "Snakes were in central Texas?"

He shakes his head. "No, they came across each other on I-10 heading into New Mexico."

"Fuck, I wonder who it was."

"He said it was some guys called Exterminator, Magnum, and Zeus. They were on a quick run to the Mexican border and managed to cross paths with the Twisted Snakes close to New Mexico. Chaos thinks they were headed for either Vegas or Cali."

"Did the Oath Keepers make it?"

"One was shot, but supposedly they killed all but two Twisted Snakes. One of the survivors headed into New Mexico, while the other escaped east."

"There's a chance we can catch one of them then."

He agrees. "There's also the possibility of the other guy going for backup."

"Holy shit, is there a plan?"

"Prez wants us keeping an eye on the surrounding routes heading into town. If we can get him incapacitated but alive, even better. The ultimate goal is to not allow him back to their clubhouse, in case they have others there as well."

"Bet. Everybody else know?"

He nods. "Yep, you are the last to show up."

"I was waiting for Leigh to go to work. I followed her to the smoothie shop before coming here."

His brows lift. "Chaos will see you're good for her soon enough."

"I have a feeling if he didn't already know, I wouldn't be near her now."

He chuckles. "You're probably right."

"And what about you? Does it bother you I'm with your sister?"

He shrugs. "It did at first. I was fucking pissed because it never crossed my mind you could be interested in her. I spoke to my mom, though, and she made me see some shit differently. Besides, I'm not sure I could deal with some prick showing up and being kissy face with her and shit. I'd probably end up burying him and she'd hate me. It works out better this way for all of us."

It's my turn to laugh. "I don't want to go there, bro. I'll get edgy just picturing her with someone else, and I need my mind right so we can catch this Snake."

"I doubt we'll see him, but let's ride."

We hop on our bikes and take off. It feels so fucking good to have my custom Street 750 back. She may be a 2016, but Harley wasn't fucking around when they made the motorcycle. She holds up like a true beast, one I plan to keep around for a long time, even if it is a bit uncomfortable since I've gotten taller. The bike was perfect when I was younger, but once I shot over five-ten it got a little uncomfortable on longer rides.

I follow Ruin out to a less-traveled road, one I've taken several times with my father. These less popular backroads are good for runs if only a few of you are riding. The cops are unlikely to pop you on some bullshit, versus if it's a big group of guys on a run.

He turns onto a private drive, swooping around to conceal the bikes in the shade of some tall bushes and trees. We're right at the mouth of the road but out of sight, so we can easily haul ass after someone from here. It's a long way to the actual property, so we most likely won't come across the owners or visitors while we wait. If we do, they won't say shit anyhow. This is club business, and while Uprising may be full of nosey fuckers, they also tend to keep their distance.

We toe our kickstands down, resting back on our seats. Ruin reaches into a bag, pulling free a tub of cookies.

"Where'd they come from?"

"Stopped by Centerfolds. Aspen made a bunch so I swiped them."

I flash a grin. "Nice." He holds the tub towards me and I grab a handful.

"Dick," he grumbles, not willing to share anymore. Not that I can blame him, but I'm starving.

"Anything going on at the shop?"

"Inked this sick jester last night. Thought it was going to take two sessions but I knocked it out."

"That's what's up. I need to stop in to get my KOC tatted."

He finishes a cookie and asks, "When you want it? Where?"

"Soon as possible, so whenever you're not booked. I'm not sure, probably let Leigh pick a spot for me."

He rolls his eyes. "Please, Spade, you know I'll ink you up whenever you want it. Swing by the house tomorrow around noon and I'll get the outline done at least."

"Appreciate it."

He bops his head and we sit around shooting the shit for a few more hours. On hour three, we perk up, hearing the faint roar of pipes. I chin lift towards his pocket. "Anybody hit you up?"

He shakes his head. "Nah, my shit hasn't vibrated. I told Tyra not to text unless it's an emergency today, since we're all on look out."

"Fuck, could it be?" We quietly start our engines—well, as quiet as we can so as to not spook anyone.

"We can hope. Talk about fucking luck if it's that bastard," Ruin mutters.

I agree and toe-up my kickstand, getting ready to take off. We wait, and wait, and as my impatience is beginning to claw at my insides, the rider finally swoops by. We both gun it, hauling ass to get up on the guy before he can punch it and leave us in his dust. I'm able to make out the same symbol on his patch as before and gesture to Ruin that I think it's who we're looking for. The rider picks up on us hot on his tail and gives it everything he's got.

I'm racing down the old roadway far too fast to retrieve my nine from my holster. Ruin is probably in the same predicament, so no shooting the dude to get him to slow the fuck down apparently. I want his guy something fierce, but he's not going down easy. We were only about twenty minutes outside of town when doing a leisurely fifty-five miles per hour. He's doing anything but. If I had to guess, he's pushing a hundred, and we're not on the right road for that shit. At this rate, we're going to be shooting straight through the main part of Uprising. I can see it in my mind, the people out walking by the business, them crossing the street, and then the fucking stoplight.

Christ, unless that light is green and everyone is cleared out of the way, this is going to end badly, I already know it. I tap my emergency call button and it links me to Dad. His voice is loud in my earpiece. "You all right?"

"We're behind him."

"I'll head to you."

"No, he's going to town. He's going too fast."

"Be safe, Sterling. Nothing is more important than your life. Love you, son." He hangs up, not wanting to distract me. Dad has always been psycho about distractions along with drinking then riding. He didn't care if I was plastered, so long as I didn't ride or drive after.

I concentrate on the road, on keeping in control of my bike. I can hear Ruin beside me, but I don't dare look over at him right now. He's probably worrying about the same thing as I am. We'll race right by the diner, Mooney's, Jupiter's, and two gas stations, amongst other small businesses. This is a fucking shitstorm on the horizon.

My adrenaline thrums through me, my heart beating double-time. My teeth are clenched, my muscles tight as I attempt to run down one of the fuckers who were the reason I dipped my bike before. We need to question him and find out what the fuck his club's been doing riding through territories and having random shootouts with other clubs. Do they have a death wish or something? The fuckers are crazy. They come across a big enough club and they'd be toast in a blink. Hell, they would've been had they not caught the three of us out by ourselves. That seems to be their MO though, going after a few people here and there. Bunch of fucking pussies.

A crossroad is coming up, and I see the eighteen-wheeler at the stop sign. He's not going to care how fast we're going, if he can even gauge it from that far away. For any other vehicle, it'd be plenty of time for him to get out on the road. In this case, however, it's not going to happen. I ease up on my gas, honking so Ruin will do the same. He must see it too because he and I begin to back off.

The scene in front of us plays out like a bad horror movie...The type where you can't look away in time, and you see it all play out in front of you. It's something I'll remember for the rest of my life.

There're bike pieces everywhere, as well as blood. It's so bad, the carnage. I find myself turning away as to not get nauseous at what could've been us had we not been paying better attention. People have no idea how lethal riding a motorcycle can be, and well, some just don't give a fuck. They're the ones who usually end up on the side of the road like this guy.

Ruin strides towards me after we've pulled off to the side and he's checked everything over. "The driver's fine, just shaken up. It's Gary from Uptown transport."

I offer a jerky nod. I'd assumed it was. We see the company a lot. "I saw it, man...before we were even close, I knew it. I wish I could've stopped it from playing out like that...somehow."

He dips his chin. "I know. As soon as you honked, I watched it play out in my mind too. Good lookin' out."

"Yeah, not good enough apparently."

"Hey, that asshole was fucking crazy. We both know it. The sheriff's department will be out here soon. You need to go."

"I'm not leaving you alone with this shitshow. They'll have questions no doubt."

His brows rise as he nods adamantly. "Yeah, you are. I know you have a few pieces in your bags. You can't get popped over being in the wrong place at the wrong time."

Fuck. He's right. I usually have one or two firearms filed down and hella illegal in my bags for sale. I'd just put in a few new handguns from our run to Louisiana. We'd brought them a load, but I also picked up a few smaller pieces that I knew would sell quickly around here, and the cops would pop me if they found them. "I'll figure it out."

"Bullshit, Spade. I have my sister's ass to think off. She'll be on me like a pissed-off chihuahua that I let you get popped when it wasn't needed. Bash will be here soon anyhow. I'm guessing you called him already."

I nod. He knows me too well. "What if they take you in?"

"Bash will have my back. Besides, you know Chaos won't let me stay locked up."

"Fuck!" I curse. "I don't like this shit."

"Go! If you wait then the law will know you were here. Hurry the fuck up. I'll catch you at the club when this is cleaned up."

I bump his fist and eventually take off. He's right, if I waited any longer then the cops would've shown up and they probably would've searched all of us. I'd go to jail in a heartbeat on weapons charges, and I help bring in too much cash for the club to get popped when it's not necessary.

Another rider approaches a beat later, and I realize it's Dad. I swear I see the relief on his face. I lift my fingers to him and gesture behind me as I pass. He lifts a few fingers in response, and I head straight for the club to catch Chaos up on everything. I'm sure he'll have the CliffsNotes version from Ruin, but he'll want every detail; it's just how he is.

When you learn to survive without anyone,
you can survive anything.
- www.livelifehappy.com

Leigh

"I can't believe you two are together-together. Finally," Magnolia comments as she drinks from the smoothie I just finished making for her. I'm quite sure at this point I make the best smoothies in town. I may be a bit biased, but everyone always asks for more eventually.

I sip from mine, having just got off work and sat in the booth across from her. My feet are tired, but I'm excited to spend some time with Sterling. "I know. I'm still randomly pinching myself to make sure I'm not dreaming."

"When you came back from Atlanta and told me you two were a legit couple, I'll admit, I was skeptical at first. I thought it was going to be more of you getting your heartbroken, but things seem to be good with you guys. Right?"

I nod, beaming. "It's been over two weeks, and he's been wonderful to me. I always knew Sterling was a sweet guy, but it's an entirely different level now that we're together."

"I thought you were crazy for wanting him for so long, but maybe you knew what you were after all along."

I smirk. "He's one fine hunk of man meat. That's exactly what I was after," I admit, making her laugh.

"He may be good to look at, but he's crazy like the rest. He just hides it well, and those are the ones you should be scared of."

I shrug. Her comment doesn't bother me in the slightest because I'm used to their brand of crazy. "I started bringing some of my stuff to his place, He hasn't complained, so that's a win."

"Oh Lord, should've known you'd already be leaving a toothbrush on his sink. Marking your territory?" she teases. It's partially true though. Sterling is mine, and I'll do whatever I have to, to make sure everyone knows as much.

"Maybe." I grin.

Her brow kicks up. "What are you going to do about the porn? There's no way you can be jealous if that's his job."

"Oh, I had a very 'come to Jesus' talk with him and my brother."

"Why am I not surprised?" She chuckles, shaking her head. "Good for you."

"I told them both that the only way Sterling is doing any porn from here on out is if it's with me."

Her mouth drops. "No way! Damn, girl, I knew you had that feistiness in you somewhere! Start calling you Luscious Leigh."

I burst out in a laugh, not expecting the last little comment from her. "That is not going to be my name! And I'm not a stripper down at Centerfolds, thank you very much."

"Wait, they agreed?! I can't believe it! And those killer hips of yours would get you hired at Centerfolds in a heartbeat. Those curves are what men dream of."

I hold my hands up, still quietly chuckling a bit. Usually, she's the one saying stuff to catch me off guard, and I thoroughly enjoyed having the drop on her this round. "They didn't exactly agree to me doing porn, but they did agree that I'd be the only one with Sterling if he does any more porn. And I'll only be doing dances for my man. These hips better hold all of his interest."

"How's he going to make money though? Plus, he has a lot of fans. I agree with you on him not sleeping with anyone else, but he shouldn't stop completely."

I can't exactly admit to her that he'll be taking on more club responsibilities and take a cut home from it. Even I'm not supposed to know much about it. I only do because I'm a club brat, the prez's daughter, and with Sterling. Most members tell their women squat when it comes to club business. "We're going to play around with some different ideas and see if we can find something that works. Ruin isn't on board with me in videos, but if I was to be in a full suit to whip Sterling or something fun and kinky, then he can deal."

"Holy shit, it's like dominatrix Barbie and biker Ken on camera." She giggles, and I can't help but follow along. "I never dreamed in a million years we'd be having this conversation."

I nod, my eyes wide as I say, "Trust me, me either!"

"I'm going to live vicariously through you with this whole 'maybe porn scenario.' I hope you realize as much."

"I figured." I wink and she grins. We finish our smoothies, and I hug her as we say our good-byes. She has homework to do for her classes, and I can't wait to see my man. It's still surreal thinking of him as mine. For a beat, I wasn't sure it was ever going to happen, and now, I can't imagine my life any other way. I've never been happier than I have been these past two weeks.

I had a heart-to-heart with my parents and they agreed to back off and give me some space. I still want to see them a lot, but there have to be some boundaries in place. Once I brought it up to them, they respected my wishes and told me their feelings on it as well. Eventually, we reached an agreement we are all okay with.

The only person with access to tracking my phone is Sterling, and in retrospect, I can with his as well. He promised to only track mine for safety, and I promised I'd check with Bash before I just show up at a random location in case it's dangerous. Luckily, I've known Bash my entire life, and if I thought Ster was at a woman's place, Bash would be more than willing to drive over there with me while I lay into them both.

I promised to text my dad a lot, especially when I work nights, so he won't worry so much. My mom's the most understanding. I was kind of surprised, but she just mentioned that she knows I'm in good hands. I'm glad she has faith in me and in Sterling, but I was expecting a little reluctance from her. Ruin has always been protective over me, and I doubt that'll never change, but he's also always been upfront with me. I know if he has a concern, he'll bring it to me straight away so we can deal with it. Sterling did warn he'd take back his house key, though, if Ruin decides to barge into the bedroom unannounced again.

Sterling's patched and we've been spending a lot of time at the club, which I love. I get to be around my family and extended family so it's always a good time. One thing it has brought to the center of my attention, however, is the prospect of being an ol' lady. Sterling and I haven't been official for long, but I still can't help but wonder if he'll make me his ol' lady. I want to be, one hundred percent I do. I won't mention it though. I don't want to push already when we're in a really good spot. I've been asking the others how long it took until they were asked to be ol' ladies and it wasn't too long for them. I'm hoping that stays true in my case as well.

"Hey sexy pants," I greet as Sterling wraps me in his strong hold.

"Boo," he murmurs, leaning in to kiss me tenderly. "How was your day?"

"Same as usual. Magnolia came to chill for a bit."

"Sweet. Nobody sketchy coming around?"

I shake my head. "You need to stop worrying so much. You said there were only two guys from that bad club and that one went west, right?"

He squeezes me tightly before relaxing his arms and saying, "One, and I don't care how many fuckers are out there. I still need to know every single day that you didn't have an issue."

I offer him a soft smile. "You realize there'll be days I have that aren't good, right?"

He shrugs. "Doesn't mean I won't try like hell to make sure that doesn't happen."

He's seriously the sweetest man I've ever met before. He may be a bit wild and rough around the edges at times, but Sterling has a heart of gold, and it's all for me. Waiting for him, no matter how long it took, was the best decision I ever made. "I love you, Sterling. I always have and I always will."

His smile blooms as he leans in, his forehead lightly resting against mine. His silver gaze meets mine, as his scent envelops me in comfort. "And I love you, Leigh. Never have a doubt in your mind about that. You're mine, baby." His mouth meets mine in a slow, passionate kiss that has my toes curling. I want to peel him out of his cut and jeans, but I can't yet.

Loud catcalls emerge, and I pull away, cheeks red. He chuckles, his face lit up with happiness as he yells at the brothers to mind their business. This is exactly where I was meant to end up—in Sterling's arms, surrounded by friends and family. In love and happy.

I love seeing people walking by with little smiles on their face because something small happened that made them happy. Maybe they got a cute text, maybe they got laid, maybe they killed a man. You will never know.

-Pinterest Meme

Sterling

We got lucky with everything, though I won't worry Leigh by telling her that. Many stories don't end up like ours. We caught one hell of a break with the Twisted Snakes coming across the Oath Keepers. Had they been able to either recruit new members or get some backup involved, there's no telling what could've happened the next time they rolled through Uprising. Leigh made an easy target being Prez's daughter, living alone without Duke to help keep her safe. Once the Snake came back to town, it was effortless to convince Prez to be on board with

Leigh moving into my place. The trailer park is off the beaten path, and I can protect Leigh. My life is hers when it comes to her safety being involved.

Everybody around this place knows how much I love that girl, and those feelings get stronger with each day. It's been a few months since everything went down, and we've been settling into our version of normal. I look at her now and I don't know how I ever missed her devotion towards me, along with her unquestionable attraction. On the upside, once word spread around town that she's my girlfriend, the majority of the asshats backed off her. Sure, I'd always been right at her back, ready to defend her, but now I can shout it from the rooftops that she's actually mine.

"Hey, Boo," I greet her as soon as she steps her sexy body through the club doors. She's in my arms in a flash, wearing a pleased smile. Having her this close makes everything feel right in the world, even when it's not. She was meant to be mine, by my side. There's no doubt about it in my mind. Magnolia traipses in behind her, taking her sweet-ass time. "Didn't know you were bringing your hoodlum friend with you."

She grins, her eyes sparkling with humor as she smacks my chest. "She's not a hoodlum."

"Mm, if you say so," I tease and am rewarded with a delicious kiss. I could stay like this for forever with her and never get enough.

Magnolia butts in, "Ugh, save it for later. I'm tired of you two always sucking face." I flip her off behind Leigh, so my sweet sugar doesn't see it. I still can't stand Magnolia much, but I tolerate her for Leigh. She's a good friend to her, and that's all I care about.

"Where's Saint?" Magnolia asks, and I roll my eyes.

"Not with you," I mutter automatically.

"Fuck off," she grumbles, peering around the club.

"Pretty sure he's at Porn Kings getting his dick sucked." He's here, but I want to fuck with her a bit, since she has a hot spot for him.

"Still no patch yet?" Leigh asks, and I shake my head. "Not yet, but I have a feeling it'll be soon for him. He's a good dude and would fit well with the Kings." She nods, rubbing her fingertips over my member patch.

"He'd fit well with me," Magnolia comments, undeterred by my earlier comment.

"Sorry to break it to you, but I'm pretty sure he's met someone."

"Who?" They both peer at me.

I shrug. "Not any of my business or yours."

Magnolia sends Leigh a look, silently claiming she thinks I'm full of shit. She can think that all she wants to, but it's the truth. I learned long ago to keep my nose outta shit, and I like it that way. Besides, I didn't ask Leigh to come to the club to discuss prospects or brothers, but something else. It's taken a while to get Chaos on board, but I wanted to have his support. After this step, the only thing left is buying a ring, and I'm not ready for marriage yet. Not that I'm not committed. I am, one hundred percent. It's why I want her here tonight and why we live together.

Ruin comes strolling out from the back, Tyra by his side. That's another thing I enjoy about having Leigh now: I'm no longer feeling like a third wheel around my best friend and his chick. "Damn, it's taking you long enough." he says, his gaze flashing between me and Leigh.

"I just got off," she smiles.

"Gross, not trying to hear that shit. You're my sister."

She huffs, "Do you guys ever stop?"

Grinning, I shake my head. "We never stop giving each other

shit, babe. You should've realized this by now."

"Yeah, yeah...So what's going on tonight, anything?"

I'd asked her to come here instead of home, but didn't give her any details. I chin lift to Ruin, and he takes the hint. "Come outside with us, Magnolia," he orders, not giving her any room to argue.

Leigh's curious gaze takes me in after they've gone. "Is everything okay?"

"It's more than okay," I reply, taking her hands in mine. "Just wanted to ask you something."

"Oh?"

"You know damn well that I love you and I'd do anything for you."

She nods. "You've made me feel that way from the moment you said you were done wasting time away from me."

"Good. Well, I wanted you to come here, 'cause it felt right that I ask you here."

"Okay?" she draws the word out, brows bunched.

"Will you be my ol' lady, and not just my girl?"

Her face transforms with the wide smile overtaking her mouth. She does this adorable squeal thing and jumps at me. I manage to catch her before she plows me over and her legs wrap around my hips. She peppers excited kisses all over my face. "Hell yes! I thought you were never going to ask!"

I chuckle at her excitement, my heart pounding with the way she always manages to twist me up in knots over her. "Love you, Boo," I murmur, eagerly accepting all the affection she's showering me with. I've never met another woman quite like Leigh, and I'm one lucky sonofabitch to be able to call her mine.

I wrap my arms around her tightly and begin to walk towards the back of the clubhouse. "Where are you taking us? We can't fuck here. My father will know somehow."

"Damn right I will," Chaos booms, making her jump.

I can't help but laugh. I know her ass is going to be flaming with embarrassment. "I'm taking you out back. Everyone's waiting on us to celebrate."

"They all knew?" she asks, eye level while in my grip.

"I knew," Chaos grumbles, tossing her a smirk. "Boy was smart enough to talk to me first. I gave him a little shit and told the brothers about it. Made him sweat it that you'd say no."

"Dad!" she exclaims, but I smile and shake my head.

"Nah, it was fine. Everything worked out in the end, and I have you."

"Yes, you do," she promises, and I tote her outside.

Everyone's kicking back, enjoying some beer and barbecue. When they notice us come out, they all start cheering, making my girl's cheeks flame all over again. She's fucking adorable. I set her down next to a long table, reaching for the small piece of leather.

"Is that..." she trails off, eyes growing wide.

I nod, holding it out for her to see. "Your vest, Boo. It's official, you're my ol' lady." She tears up, and I can't help but bring her closer to me again, ready to fix whatever's made her upset. "Tell me so I can fix it."

She shakes her head, her lower lip moving with a slight tremble. "I always knew this was how it was meant to be," she confesses, and my chest swells with love.

She's right. Now that we're together, I couldn't imagine any other outcome for my future. She's strong and sweet, exactly the type of woman I needed and had no idea. Dad wasn't kidding saying I'd get sucker-punched out of nowhere. Leigh came at me like a wrecking ball, and it took far too long for me to see what was right in front of me. I'll never make that mistake again. She's all mine.

Thank you

Thank you for reading Sterling and supporting my work. Because of you, I'm able to stand on my own two feet. Sometimes in life we realize we can only truly depend on ourselves, even if we've previously learned the same lesson many moons ago. It's okay to forget it and be reminded. Sometimes we need a swift kick to the ass to get us back where we need to be. Well, I've found my footing again and I don't plan to slip anytime soon. Here's to strong women.

Women who will stand up for themselves and say I deserve respect.

Because you do.

Keep kicking ass.

#BeYourOwnHero #WeFuckingROAR

Acknowledgments

My husband –I love you, and I'm thankful for you.

My boys – You're my whole world. I love you both, this never changes. I can't express how grateful I am for your support and belief in me. You are quick to tell me that my career makes you proud and that I make you proud. As far as mom wins go, that one takes the cake, even if I do send 'mom memes'. I love you with every beat of my heart, and I will forever.

My Dogs - You guys are assholes, but I love you so much it makes my heart ache. Please stop barking and chugging water when I'm trying to write.

Women that inspire – Hilary Storm, I love you, woman! Thank you for being my friend.

Editor - Editing Done Write –I'm so grateful! Thank you for pouring hours into my passion and being wonderful to me. Thank you for your amazing support, especially on such short notice.

CT Cover Creations – I can always count on you and that means so much. Thank you for all of your hard work and the kindness you don't ever hesitate to share with me. Your designs are superb and your professionalism is on another level entirely. You set the bar high with designers and you've completely spoiled me. Thank you!

Formatting by N. E. Henderson – Thank you so much for making my book look professional and beautiful. I genuinely appreciate it and the kindness you've shown me.

My Blogger Friends – YOU ARE AMAZING! You take a

new chance on me with each book and in return, share my passion with the world. You never truly get enough credit, and I'm forever grateful!

My Readers – I love you. You make my life possible, thank you. I can't wait to meet many of you this year and in the future. To those of you leaving me the awesome spoiler-free reviews, you motivate me to keep writing. For that, I will forever be grateful, as this is my passion in life.

And as always, ADOPT DON'T SHOP! Save a life today and adopt from a rescue or your local animal shelter. #ProudDobermanMom #LastHopeDobermanRescue

Also by Sapphire

Oath Keepers MC Series

Exposed

Relinquish

Forsaken Control

Friction

Sweet Surrender – free short story

Oath Keepers MC Hybrid Series

Princess

Love and Obey – free short story

Daydream

Baby

Chevelle

Cherry

Heathen

(next book coming fall 2021)

Russkaya Mafiya Series

Secrets

Corrupted

Corrupted Counterparts – free short story

Unwanted Sacrifices

Undercover Intentions

Dirty Down South Series

Freight Train

3 Times the Heat

2 Times the Bliss

The Vendetti Famiglia

The Vendetti Empire - part 1

The Vendetti Queen - part 2

The Vendetti Seven – part 3

The Vendetti Coward – part 4

Harvard Academy Elite

Little White Lies

Ugly Dark Truth

Royal Bastards MC Texas

Opposites Attract

Kings of Carnage MC Series

Bash – Vice President

Sterling - Prospect

The Chicago Crew

Gangster

Mad Max

Complete Standalones

Gangster

Unexpected Forfeit

The Main Event – free short story

Oath Keepers MC Collection

Russian Roulette

Tease – Short Story Collection

Oath Keepers MC Hybrid Collection

Vendetti Duet

Harvard Academy Elite

Viking - free newsletter short story

Dirty Down South Collection

About the Author

Sapphire Knight is a Wall Street Journal and USA Today Bestselling Author of Secrets, Exposed, Relinquish, Corrupted, Forsaken Control, Unwanted Sacrifices, Friction, Unexpected Forfeit, Russian Roulette, Princess, Freight Train (1st Time Love), Gangster, Undercover Intentions, Daydream, Princess, Chevelle, 3 Times the Heat, Baby, The Vendetti Empire, The Vendetti Queen, Cherry, Little White Lies, Ugly Dark Truth, Harvard Academy Elite, 2 Times the Bliss, Heathen, Bash, Opposites Attract, The Vendetti Seven, The Vendetti Coward, Mad Max, and Sterling. The series are called Russkaya Mafiya, Oath Keepers MC, Ground and Pound, Dirty Down South, Harvard Academy, Kings of Carnage MC VP & Prospect, The Chicago Crew, and Royal Bastards MC Texas.

Her books all reflect on what she loves to read herself.
Sapphire's a Texas girl who's crazy about football. She's always had a passion for writing. She originally studied psychology and feels that it's added to her drive in writing.

Sapphire is the proud mom of two handsome boys. She's been married to the love of her life, an Army veteran, for sixteen years. When she's not busy in her writing cave, she's playing with her three Doberman Pinschers. She loves to donate to help animals and watch a good action movie.

Stay up to date with Wall Street Journal and USA Today Bestselling Author Sapphire Knight

www.authorsapphireknight.com

Made in the USA
Columbia, SC
18 February 2025